# GIFT
# FROM
# THE MIKADO

by ELIZABETH P. FLEMING

*Illustrated by Janet Smalley*

*Philadelphia*
THE WESTMINSTER PRESS

Library of Congress Catalog Card Number: 58–5129

WEEKLY READER

*Children's Book Club*

Edition, 1958

PRINTED IN THE UNITED STATES OF AMERICA
AMERICAN BOOK–STRATFORD PRESS, INC., NEW YORK

**Weekly Reader**

# Children's Book Club

**EDUCATION CENTER • COLUMBUS 16, OHIO**

*Presents*

# GIFT
# FROM
# THE MIKADO

*By*

ELIZABETH P. FLEMING

# 1 . .

## The Bicycle

"Come quick!" shouted Fred. "Father's bicycle has come from America!"

Ernest and Daisy dropped what they were doing and rushed out of the house. Kobi and Akio, the Japanese menservants, were right behind them, and O Yuki, the housemaid, who never wanted to miss any excitement. Even Mother left her work to hurry after them.

Outside, a large packing case had just been delivered, and around it stood a crowd of curious Japanese. For this was in the 1890's, a long time ago, when foreigners were still a novelty in Japan, and it always seemed worth-while to see what strange, outlandish thing a foreigner might be up to.

O Yuki pushed her way through the crowd. "Poate-san," she cried to Father. She was really saying, " Honorable Mr. Poate." " Poate-san, has the honorable bicycle arrived?"

" It's the bicycle all right," said Father. He turned to one of the servants. " Kobi-san," he said, " please bring me the tool chest." Kobi ran eagerly to obey.

" See," said Father to the children, pointing to the

7

big, black lettering on the crate. " It says, ' Mass., U.S.A.'
It has come all the way from America."

" I wish it said Ohio," remarked Mother, who had
come from Ashtabula and was always on the lookout for
anything from Ohio.

" Well, it's American anyway," said Father. " Now
where is Kobi, I wonder? Kobi-san," he raised his voice,
" where are you? "

Kobi appeared in the doorway. " So sorry, Poate-san,"
he said to Father. " Cannot find tool chest."

Father strode to the door. " Where are you looking for
it? " he asked, for Kobi was anxiously staring at the ceiling.

" Not here, Poate-san," he said. " So sorry."

" There it is," said Father, pointing to the shelf in the
corner. " Right where it's always been."

There was no use scolding Kobi. He could never find
anything. And no wonder, for he always looked at the
ceiling for it.

Carrying the tool chest between them, Father and Kobi
went back to the bicycle. The packing case was wonder-
fully stout. Every nail was driven in right to the very
head and squeaked stubbornly as it was pulled out. It
took a long time, but at last there was the bicycle in all its
shining newness. Everyone sighed in admiration.

" Hold it," directed Father to Kobi and Akio, " while
I put these clips on." Quickly he adjusted the clips to
keep his pants out of the wheels, while Kobi and Akio,
proud but apprehensive, held the bicycle upright. Their
legs were braced ready for anything. Who knew but that
the strange machine might take off by itself if they weren't
on guard?

" Now then," said Father when he was ready, " just watch. If I head for the canal, turn me back."

At that everyone looked at the canal, which ran very wide and very deep beside the footpath.

" Oh, don't ride the bicycle! " cried Daisy.

But Father wasn't listening. He climbed to the seat of the bicycle and put his feet on the pedals.

" All right," he said.

At the words, Kobi and Akio leaped back, letting go of the bicycle, and Father and the machine, not prepared for such prompt action, fell down with a bang.

" Are you hurt? " cried Mother.

" Of course not," said Father, picking himself up. He turned to the men. " Not so fast about letting go. Maybe you'd better hold on and run along beside me until I get

the hang of the thing. And mind the canal," he finished.

They were off again, the bicycle wobbling from side to side, while the little Japanese strained to keep it upright. Then all of a sudden it headed straight for the canal. Faster and faster it went, Father's legs working like pistons, and nearer and nearer it came to the brink. Kobi and Akio were running now. There wasn't a minute to lose. At the very last minute Kobi threw himself down in front of the wheel, and the ride ended in a tangle of legs and arms.

Father got up laughing. " Well done, Kobi-san," he said.

The crowd of watching Japanese drew a collective hissing breath. They had not known how to take this strange spectacle. But if Poate-san could laugh, they could too. They giggled happily.

Father got on the bicycle again, and things seemed to go better. " I think I've got it," he said after a while. " Stand away, men."

For a moment the bicycle on its own wavered precariously. Then the wheels straightened and began to spin rhythmically. Away sailed Father with majestic speed.

" *Banzai! Banzai!* " shrilled the Japanese.

And, " Hurray! Hurray! " shouted the children.

When Father came back, he was loud in his praises. " She skims along like a bird," he said. " It's the greatest invention since the steam engine. I wish I'd ordered one with a high front wheel. A tall man can work up speed with a high wheel, because his legs are longer."

Mother shook her head. " You are going quite fast enough," she told him.

Every day after that, Father rode his bicycle into
Tokyo, where he taught at the university. He was working too with a committee that was revising the Japanese
translation of the Bible. It meant many a long trip into
the city, but with the bicycle to ride, it was child's play,
he said. Every morning a little group of Japanese gathered to see him start off, and every night they were there
to mark his return with indrawn breaths of admiration.

"I wish I could have a bicycle," said Fred, who was
the oldest, going on eleven.

"Me too," said Ernest, who was two years younger.

"And me too," said Daisy, though she was only half
past six and really too little for a bicycle.

"I think an American express cart would be the thing
for you," said Father. "Study the catalogue and see what
you can find."

There was everything in the world in the mail-order
catalogue: tables and chairs, whatnots and bicycles, bug-
gies, and, sure enough, express wagons. The children
spent hours poring over the pictures. At last they chose
an express wagon that seemed to be the very best. "Chain
Lightning" was its name. It was varnished yellow, with
name and decorations in red, the catalogue told them.

Father sat down to write a letter to the mail-order
house in Chicago.

"When will it come?" the children asked.

"In good time," said Father. "Remember, it's a long
way to America. The bicycle was slow in coming, and
'Chain Lightning' won't be as fast as its name. Be pa-
tient and someday it will surprise you."

" How much longer do we have to wait for the express wagon? " Fred asked Father some days later.

" Well," said Father, " it will take four or five weeks for the letter to get there. Then the wagon must be crated before it can be sent. A few months may get it here, with good luck."

The children groaned. " So long? We might as well give up," they said dismally.

" You shouldn't complain," said Father. " Travel is much faster than it used to be. When I was a boy and first went out to Hong Kong from England, it took us one hundred and ten days to Hong Kong. Of course, that was before the Suez Canal was opened. We had to sail around Africa past the Cape of Good Hope, which was named the Cape of Storms — a good name, too," he added. " Get your map and I'll show you."

Ernest ran for the atlas.

" Here we are," said Father, and he traced the course for them. " And now, see how much time is saved by using the canal." And he followed the new course with his finger.

" I was only seventeen then," said Father. " I had been sick and the doctor recommended a sea voyage. What a long voyage that was! The hens on board didn't get enough lime in their diet, and after a while they laid eggs without shells — only a membrane around them."

" Where did the chickens live? " asked Ernest.

" Below deck," said Father. " I used to go down to visit them every day. I even gave them names. The rooster was Hilkiah, after the high priest in the Bible. Do you remember Hilkiah? " he asked. When no one answered,

Father said Fred could look it up in the concordance by and by.

" Poor Hilkiah," said Father. " Someone carelessly left the door of the hencoop open one day, and Hilkiah got out. He sailed right over the ship's side into the sea."

"Did the ship turn about and rescue him? " asked Ernest. " Did you throw out a life preserver? "

" Well, no," said Father. " They could hardly do that for a rooster — even Hilkiah."

The children sighed. " I suppose not," said Ernest.

When it was time for evening prayers, Father told Fred to look up Hilkiah in the concordance and they would have the story for the Bible lesson. Fred found it after a while. " Second Kings, chapter 22," he read off.

" Good," said Father. " Now find the place in the Bible." Then he went to the door. In a high, singsong voice he gave the Japanese call to prayers.

Soon all the household were assembled. Father read the story of the finding of the Book of the Law in the days of good King Josiah. Then Mother played a hymn on the reed organ and they sang, Mother's voice rising sweet and clear above the others. Kobi and Akio and O Yuki, the housemaid, loved to sing, though their voices were very nasal. No matter, the happiness on their faces made up for the music, Mother always said.

They finished their prayers with the words all Christians in Japan repeated each night: " Deliver us from fire and earthquake." For fire was a constant menace with the flimsy houses, and earthquakes an ever-present danger.

After prayers Mother saw the children off to bed and fixed the netting so not a mosquito could get in.

## 2..

# The Shadow with the Sword

Mother *looked* up from the letter she was reading. " Mrs. Barker writes she isn't well and is going to retire. She wants to visit us before she sails for America, and would next week be convenient."

Father hesitated a minute. " We must have her, of course," he said. Then he added quickly, " Yes, do tell her to come."

" Who's Mrs. Barker? " Fred wanted to know.

" A missionary we used to know before any of you were born," said Mother.

" Why don't you want her to come? " asked Ernest, who always seemed to know what people were thinking.

" We didn't say that," said Mother. " Only she's such a capable woman," she burst out. " But very good," she added. " I do hope you children will be on your best behavior while she's here."

" Yes," said Father, " for the honor of the family."

The children nodded soberly.

" I'm sorry she's sick," said Father. " Does she say what is the matter? "

" Only that it seems to be a sort of breakdown. She says

14

she's never recovered from the shock of her husband's death. Poor woman."

" What happened to him? " asked Fred.

" He was killed by a robber," said Father.

" A real robber? " asked the children.

" Yes," said Father. " Of course that was some time ago. Things are better now. But at that time, the police weren't very effective. This robber had the whole city terrified. He simply broke into any house he chose, and no one seemed able to catch him. Besides, it was danger-ous to try, because he always carried a sword."

" O-oh! " breathed the children.

" Well," Father went on, " in the middle of the night Mr. Barker woke up to see a man with a sword in the act of lifting the mosquito netting around the bed. I sup-pose poor Barker did what any man in the circumstances would have done. He jumped up and tackled the robber. But Barker was unarmed and no match for the man. The robber killed him. Poor Mrs. Barker tried to help her hus-band and lost two fingers from her right hand. It was a terrible thing. She never gave in, though. All these years she's kept up by sheer will power. At last she's broken, poor soul. And no wonder."

" What became of the robber? " asked Fred.

" That's another story," said Father. " Mother will have to tell that, because Mother is the heroine."

Mother laughed a little at that. " This part of the story happened a good many months after Mr. Barker was killed. No one had seen or heard a thing of the robber after he escaped that night. Everyone hoped he had left the city because he was afraid after murdering a foreigner. People began to feel easy again.

"Then one day I went to a different part of the city to make some calls with a Mrs. Ishii, a Japanese Christian worker. As it was a long way, I decided beforehand that I would stay all night at Mrs. Ishii's house. It was just as well, for by the time the last call was made it was getting late. As we went along the darkening streets I felt very nervous. I hadn't been long enough in Japan to be used to being stared at. I didn't like the way everyone we met stopped to look at me.

"'Let's hurry,' I said to Mrs. Ishii. For she was taking such tiny steps we seemed to be scarcely moving. Clop-clop, footsteps sounded behind us, and when I looked around there was a crowd of people following us."

"Where was Father?" Daisy interrupted.

"I didn't know him then," Mother explained. "Well," she went on, "I thought we would never get to Mrs. Ishii's house. But we did, of course, with the curious crowd following. Even after we went inside, they stood about, peeking through the cracks between the paper screens. Mrs. Ishii was a widow who lived with her son. But her son was away. We were alone. We closed the heavy wooden shutters for the night, shutting out the curious crowd, and after a while they all went away.

"Mrs. Ishii had a nice house with a little loftlike room upstairs reached by a straight ladder of planks, and there we were to sleep. When we went up to bed, I suggested that we leave a light burning downstairs, though I didn't say why.

"I could see that Mrs. Ishii wasn't worried a bit, and I wasn't going to admit that I was. Very soon Mrs. Ishii went to sleep, but I lay there watching the patch of light

shining on the stair wall from the lamp downstairs. I
heard a faint noise. It sounded like the sliding of a door.
I sat up quietly and listened. There wasn't a sound, but
I knew there was someone downstairs. As I stared at the
light on the wall I saw something move. The shadow of
a man with a sword moved up the stairs toward our
room."

"What did you do?" cried Ernest. "Hurry, Mother!
Tell us!"

"I couldn't do anything," Mother said. "But I began
to pray right out loud, and without a sound the shadow
moved down the wall until I couldn't see it any more."

"What happened then?" Fred's voice shook with excitement.

"Well, by this time Mrs. Ishii was awake and we
listened, but everything was perfectly quiet. We half
hoped the robber had gone away. But I didn't dare trust
to it. As long as he knew we were awake I thought he
wouldn't risk coming upstairs. I began to talk. Mrs. Ishii
tried to answer me, but she was so afraid that she couldn't
speak. So I talked to myself. I recited Bible verses. I sang
hymns, on and on, without stopping. Once I got so tired
that I must have dozed, for when I looked at the wall,
there was the shadow again, coming up the stairs. I began
talking again. Hour after hour I kept it up, all night long,
until, at last, morning came and the robber went away."

Daisy pulled at Mother's dress. "Mother, did he come
back another night?" she asked.

"No, dear," said Mother. "That was the last time he
ever broke into a house. The police caught him that very
morning and took him off to prison, where he never had
a chance to do harm again."

The children sat silent for a minute, then Ernest spoke. "There's that proverb in my copybook," he said. "'The pen is mightier than the sword.' I think the tongue is mightier than the sword too. At least, Mother's tongue is."

"Well said, Ernest," remarked Father. "That's a good proverb."

Mother blushed with pleasure, but she shook her head.

"Mightiest of all was God," she said, "who took care of us."

"Now remember," warned Mother, "Mrs. Barker isn't used to children and she's not well. Try to be very good. And at table mind your manners. Don't talk with your mouths full. Better still, don't talk. Let the grown-ups do that."

"I'm sorry," said Father, coming in. "I couldn't get any butter. There isn't a bit in the city and won't be until the next ship docks."

"Oh, dear," said Mother, "there's only the tiniest pat left."

"Never mind," Father told her. "Mrs. Barker hasn't lived all these years in Japan without having seen many a butter shortage."

"I'll put what little butter there is on a side plate at her place," Mother decided. "She probably won't notice what the rest of us have."

Mother was going to warn the children not to ask for butter, but at that moment a commotion broke out in the street, and they ran out to see what was happening.

It was Mrs. Barker, riding in a ricksha and looking very stylish in a dress with big sleeves and a hat with a plume. But her face was thin and sad. Mother gave her a kiss, and the two women went into the house arm in arm, while Father followed with Mrs. Barker's bag, and Daisy trailed along at the rear.

" You have a very pretty hat," said Daisy shyly.

" Why, thank you, dear," Mrs. Barker said. She turned to Mother. " The plume is a present from the Mothers' Group," she said. " They wanted me to look nice when I went home to America. Mrs. Ishii chose the plume and sewed it on for me."

" Is that Mother's Mrs. Ishii? " asked Daisy.

" Yes," said Mrs. Barker. " She sent her love to her ' beloved teacher.' " And she smiled at Mother,

" Dear Mrs. Ishii," said Mother.

While they were talking, the Swiss clock began to strike. Mother loved the clock, even though it always stopped ticking at the slightest earthquake, and with earthquakes so common it never kept good time. It was a miracle to hear it striking exactly at noon. Mother felt quite proud.

" By the time you're ready, dinner will be ready too,"

said Mother, and left Mrs. Barker in her room while she went to call the boys.

" Remember, be good," she warned again while they washed their hands.

The table looked very nice with Mother's best damask cloth and water lilies in the blue dish made like a Japanese junk. The children were quiet, and the grownups talked of old times. Everything was going well. And then Ernest spoiled it all. Mrs. Barker, who had been eating a little awkwardly with her left hand, suddenly raised her right, and he saw two stumps where fingers should have been. A horrid sickness swept over him.

" Oh," he groaned, right in the middle of Mrs. Barker's story of the Mothers' Group tea. He shut his eyes tight and held his napkin to his mouth.

" What is it? " asked Mother. She took one look at Ernest and hustled him from the room.

Mrs. Barker shook her head. Her mouth was set in a thin line.

Father tried to pretend nothing had happened. " You were telling us about the tea," he said.

Mrs. Barker looked down at her plate. " No matter."

There was an embarrassed pause, and then Father began to talk of his work on the Japanese Bible. He talked well. In spite of herself, Mrs. Barker listened.

" I'm almost finished with my work," said Father.

" And what then? " asked Mrs. Barker.

" I still have my teaching at the university," said Father.

" We have had requests for someone to go to the university in Morioka," said Mrs. Barker. " The young men there are anxious to learn English. It will have to be someone who knows the Japanese language thoroughly. You are the best we have." She looked at Father.

" Morioka," said Father thoughtfully.

" It's in the interior," said Mrs. Barker. " So far, we have touched only the port cities. There's a great opportunity waiting."

Father nodded.

Fred was looking for butter. It wouldn't be polite, of course, to interrupt the grownups to ask for some. Right beside him at Mrs. Barker's place was a small pat. He reached over and scooped it up with his knife.

Mother slipped into her place. At Father's inquiring look, she said Ernest was staying in the kitchen with O Yuki. " I think he got overexcited," she said.

" Butter, please," said Daisy.

Mother shook her head. " No, Daisy," she murmured. " There isn't any butter."

" Fred has some," Daisy persisted. " He took it off Mrs. Barker's plate."

" Why, Fred," said Father, surprised into speech. " That was the last butter in the city. It was for Mrs. Barker."

Everyone looked at Fred. " I didn't know," he said, his face very red.

" We were talking about Morioka," Mrs. Barker said stiffly.

After dinner Ernest appeared in the doorway. " I'm all right now," he said. " May I go out to play? "

Mother nodded, and the children went outdoors. Mother and Mrs. Barker settled down for a talk. But not for long. Soon shouts came from the yard, growing louder and louder by the minute.

# 3..

## "Chain Lightning"

In a moment the children were back. " It's come! The express wagon's come! "

There was no waiting this time for Kobi to find the tool chest. Fred and Ernest brought it almost before Father had paid the carrier. Father pointed out " Chicago, Ill., U.S.A." in black letters on the crate and said they could look it up in the atlas. But nobody cared about geography just then, especially when Father pried off the lid and they could get a glimpse of the wagon. It was varnished yellow and the wheels were red, as the catalogue had promised. There was a zigzag of red along one side and the name, " Chain Lightning," in big red letters.

Father lifted it out of the crate, and without waiting a minute, Fred flung himself into the wagon.

" Make way for ' Chain Lightning,' " he shouted, and was off like a streak.

" Wait! Wait for me! " cried Ernest.

" Come back," called Father.

But Fred paid no attention to them.

" I hope he falls in the canal," Ernest said angrily.

" Now, now," said Father. But when Fred came back

22

at last, he spoke sternly. " That was very selfish," he said.

Fred hung his head. " I didn't think," he mumbled.

" The wagon belongs to all three of you," said Father. " There must be fair play. Turn and turn about. It's Ernest's turn now. To the corner and back. Then Daisy's. All according to age."

When Father spoke like that, the children knew he meant it, and for a while they played in perfect peace and quiet.

Mrs. Barker had just finished telling of her trip when angry words were heard from outside.

" Please excuse me," Mother interrupted. " Something is wrong with the children." And she hurried out.

Fred was shouting at some Japanese children who were standing by the gate. " Go home! We don't want you here."

" Fred! " cried Mother, " That's no way to talk."

" They want to ride in my wagon," said Fred. " They can't do it."

" Your wagon? " said Mother. " It's Ernest's and Daisy's too. And why shouldn't the others have rides? "

" They're only Japanese," said Fred.

Mother was horrified. " Where did you ever hear such talk? " she asked.

" Mr. Vorhees says it," said Fred, a little scared now.

Mr. Vorhees had come to Japan to make money and he despised anything that didn't help line his pockets. No one approved of Mr. Vorhees, and Fred knew it.

" I'm sorry," he said. " All the same, if we start letting them have rides, we won't have a chance ourselves."

" I think," said Mother, " that you had better go to

your room and think this over for a while. One hour by the clock," she called after him, as he started for the house.

" But what if the clock stops? " he asked anxiously.

" I'll keep track," said Mother.

She turned to Daisy and Ernest. " The children are your friends. Of course, you must share with them."

She waited until Jiro, the boy who often came to play, was started on his ride, then she turned toward the house. It was only then that she saw Mrs. Barker beside her.

Oh, dear, Mother thought. Mrs. Barker heard it all. Mother felt silly and helpless as she used to when, as a bride, she had looked on Mrs. Barker as a pattern of efficiency.

" My dear," said Mrs. Barker, " you are a slave to those children. They are growing up to be selfish and thoughtless. I say it for your own good."

" They're really good children," defended Mother. " This has been a very exciting day with a new express wagon and company too."

" Possibly," said Mrs. Barker. " But — " She broke off as a wail sounded from the bedroom, and Daisy burst into the room, the plume from Mrs. Barker's hat clutched in her hand. " I did it not meaning to," she wept. " I was looking at it and it came off."

" Oh, Daisy! " gasped Mother. Mrs. Barker didn't say anything.

Mother said at last: " I think Mrs. Ishii sewed the plume on the Japanese way, with long stitches — you know they always rip their clothes apart to wash them. I'll sew it on more stoutly," and she went for her workbasket. " How could you? " she asked Daisy, who fol-

lowed her. " We are in disgrace. Go outdoors and try to
be good enough to make up."

Yet after that, things seemed to go better. Mother
sewed on the plume at what Mrs. Barker admitted was a
more becoming angle. Father came home and they talked
of Morioka. At prayers, Mrs. Barker's alto voice made the
hymns sound very nice. At last the long day ended happily for everyone.

" I'm hungry," said Daisy.

" So am I," said Ernest.

" I'm starving," said Fred.

They were waiting breakfast for Mrs. Barker.

" Don't you think we'd better eat without her? " asked
Father.

" Perhaps she overslept," said Mother. " Poor soul, she
looks as though she needed rest."

" I hope she doesn't come," said Ernest. " Her fingers
make me sick."

" It's harder on Mrs. Barker than on anyone else," said
Father. " Remember, she lost her fingers trying to save
her husband."

" I never thought of that," said Ernest.

" You sit down and eat," said Mother. " I'll see if she's
awake."

When a faint noise answered Mother's tap, she pushed
back the sliding door and went in. Mrs. Barker lay in bed,
her hands pressed to her head.

" I'm so sorry," she groaned. " I simply can't get up.
It's one of my headaches again."

Mother tried her best to make her comfortable. She
smoothed the tumbled bed and plumped the pillows.

" Shall I bring you a little breakfast? " she asked.

" No, no," moaned Mrs. Barker. " It makes me ill to think of it."

Mother tiptoed out. " Mrs. Barker's sick," she said. " We'll have to be quiet."

The children were very good, the boys full of a new plan. " We're going to have tickets for free rides in ' Chain Lightning,' " Fred explained. " Ten tickets each day. First come, first served. I thought of it yesterday when I was sitting in my room."

After lessons the boys made the tickets of rice paper with a red-ink zigzag for lightning and a black number.

Daisy played with her doll, Kate, who had blue eyes and curly hair, and, though she wore a Japanese kimono, still looked very American.

" It's cold today," said Daisy. " Kate had better wear extra clothes." She fitted one kimono inside of another and laid the doll in them. In a minute Kate was dressed.

So much easier than our way of dressing babies, thought Mother. She looked at the children, so cheerful and happy, and wondered why they couldn't have behaved like this yesterday. Who could understand them?

All morning Mrs. Barker stayed in bed. Whenever Mother looked in, she seemed to be sleeping. Once she roused to feel someone covering her up.

" I've brought you Father's steamer shawl," whispered Daisy. " We always have it when we're sick." She tucked it carefully around Mrs. Barker and went quietly away.

Ernest found the little metal hand warmer and filled it with glowing charcoal. Then he wrapped it in a towel. " I think the *kai-ro* will help your head," he said to Mrs. Barker.

" That feels very good," she sighed thankfully, as she felt the warmth on her aching head.

It was noon when Mother brought a cup of tea. " Try to drink it," she said. " Fred has made you some toast."

" I'm dreadfully sorry there's no butter," said Fred.

" Butter wouldn't be good for me," said Mrs. Barker. " Dry toast is best for headaches."

In the afternoon Mrs. Barker came out to sit with Mother in the living room. The sun shining through the paper walls cast a mellow glow in the room. The voices of the children at play came to them faintly.

" Tickets! Tickets! " Fred was calling. " This way for tickets for a free ride on the American wonder, ' Chain Lightning.' Tickets! Get your tickets here! "

Mrs. Barker smiled. " I must take back all I said about the children," she said. " You are bringing them up to be kind and sympathetic. Each one of them came to show me attention. They are the dearest children in the world."

That night after the children had gone to bed, Mother

and Father talked more about Morioka.

" I would have to give up a good position at the university," said Father. " But there's an open field in Morioka. What do you think? "

" This is the time to go," said Mother, " while the children are young, and I can teach them. When Fred is ready for high school, it will be different. But now we can be together and happy in Morioka just as well as here."

" How would we get there? " asked Father.

" There's talk of a railroad," said Mrs. Barker. " It will come, no doubt. But now, you would have to go by ricksha. Six days perhaps. The furniture could go by native cart."

" I would want to go up first to spy out the land," said Father. " If all goes well, should we go? " he asked Mother.

They exchanged a look. " Yes," said Mother.

There were tears in Mrs. Barker's eyes. " My husband and I dreamed of going into the interior to carry on the work," she said. " I have lost him and I am an old woman, sick and alone, but now I can go home to America knowing you are carrying on in our places."

Next day Mrs. Barker went away. As she stepped into the ricksha that was to take her to the station, her face beneath the plumed hat was smiling and cheerful.

The children crowded around the ricksha.

" *Sayonara,* good-by," they called.

" Such a pretty hat," sighed Daisy, as she turned back to the house. " When I grow up, I'm going to have a hat with a plume on it."

# 4..

## The Mikado's Cabinet

Now *the days* were filled with plans for the big move.

Father was going up first. " I must find a good house for us to live in," he said. " And I must get in touch with the university authorities. Don't expect me back in less than two weeks. Boys, take care of Mother and Daisy. Fred is the man of the house until I come back."

O Yuki came to sleep in the guest room while Father was away.

Kobi brought packing cases, and Mother and O Yuki began to pack dishes.

Kobi was sad. " Morioka very far away place," he said.

The next day he did not come to work. " Where is Kobi? " Mother asked.

O Yuki did not know. Kobi did not come the next day, nor the next. Then he sent word that his old father was sick and he had to go to him.

" But he has no father," said Mother. " He is an orphan."

" Morioka is too far away for Kobi-san," said Fred.

" But why didn't he tell me so? " asked Mother. Her feelings were a little hurt.

"He didn't want to make you feel bad," said Fred. "The Japanese are a very polite people."

A few days later Akio came into the house with his hand on his stomach. "Very bad pain," he said. "Cannot work. So sorry."

"Poor Akio-san," said Mother, "I will give you peppermint for your stomach-ache." She measured a few drops into some water and added a little sugar. "Drink this," she said. "Try to keep well until Poate-san comes home. We won't ask you to go to Morioka," she added. "Only, please, stay with us until we leave."

Akio sipped the medicine and smacked his lips. He took his hand from his stomach and smiled. "Very much better," he said. There was no more talk of sickness after that. Akio felt quite well as long as he didn't have to go to Morioka.

"Are you going to leave us too?" Mother asked O Yuki a little sadly.

"Where could I go?" asked O Yuki. "Your children are my children also. I could not leave you."

O Yuki had known much trouble. She had been married to a husband who abused her, and had at last driven her from his house. In the Japanese law of those days, children belonged to the father. So poor O Yuki had to leave her little boy behind. He was Fred's age when she went away, and often as she looked at Fred tears would come to her eyes, and she would wipe them away with the long sleeve of her kimono. O Yuki was a Christian, and each night she prayed for her boy, Bunji.

"Bunji is a man now," she said to Mother. "I hope he is a good man."

" You have asked God to make him good," said Mother. " You need not fear."

At last, Father came home. He had traveled on foot, by ricksha, and on foot again. It was a long way, but much of the country was beautiful. Morioka was a busy city, untouched by foreign influence. But at the university the young men were eager to learn English. There was a great field open and waiting.

Father had taken over the house of the *daimyo*, the ruler of former times. The warlike days were over, and the house had stood empty for many years. It was a good house, spacious and pleasant. Most of the *daimyo*'s grounds were used by the city for a public park, but there was a pretty garden, and Father had found a man to tend it and to see to repairs on the house.

" You'll like it," said Father.

Now he plunged into arrangements for the journey. The larger pieces of furniture would go by native cart, the smaller with the family by ricksha. But it was hard to find ricksha runners willing to go even one day's journey. They all had good reasons for staying at home, and nothing could induce them to change their minds. Each day Father went on making inquiries, and each day he came home disappointed.

" I don't know what we are going to do," he worried. But he didn't give up. One day he brought lengths of cotton for wrapping cloths to protect the goods on the journey. " We'll be ready anyway," he said.

" But this is only plain cloth," said Fred, disappointed. The children had often seen bridal processions with a long line of bearers carrying the bride's belongings to the house of the bridegroom. Each bundle was tied in a wrapping cloth with the crest of the bride's family.

" Everyone has a crest on the cloths," said Fred.

" We don't have a crest," Father pointed out.

" But couldn't we make a crest? " asked Ernest. " Just a circle with an initial in it. Please, please, may we? "

" Why not? " said Mother. " Only work outdoors. There isn't room in the house."

So Fred spread one of the big cloths on the ground, and Ernest ran to get the India ink and the brushes in the container made of a gnarled root carved to look like an old man.

" What can we use to make a circle? " he asked.

" A dinner plate," said Fred. They put the dinner plate upside down in the middle of the cloth, and Fred, as the oldest, did the first painting. But somehow the ink wouldn't go on evenly, and when they lifted the plate, there was a big blot under the edge. Daisy leaned far over to get a better look at it.

" Look out," warned Ernest. But Daisy had leaned too far. She lost her balance and her hand went right into the ink spot, spreading it about.

" Now see what you've done," scolded the boys.

Daisy's face puckered up and she was ready to cry, but just then their friend Jiro called from the gate. They were glad to see him. He hadn't been over since the day when the express cart first came.

" What are you doing? " he asked.

They showed him. " But it isn't so easy," said Fred.

" You're holding the brush wrong," said Jiro. He took

it and in one stroke made a sweeping curve. " What is your crest? " he asked.

" Just an initial in the circle," said Fred. " Like this," and he drew a letter *P* on a piece of paper.

Jiro looked at it, then made a beautiful character in the circle.

" Is that a *P?* " asked Ernest a little doubtfully. " But say," he went on quickly, " it's very nice. Will you make it on all the wrapping cloths, Jiro-san? "

So over and over Jiro made the same character in its enclosing circle, while the others watched fascinated. They were still admiring when they noticed that people were running out of their houses and hurrying down

the street. A procession was coming, and men and women, as it passed, bowed low or knelt.

" What is it? " asked Fred. But Jiro was already on his knees.

The children watched as the procession came nearer and then stopped before their very house. When Father came out, a court official began a speech, in a high, sing-song voice.

" From the most illustrious Mikado — a token of esteem for your services in the Imperial University."

Two retainers stepped forward to place a box at Father's feet.

Then Father made a speech, and there were many bows and polite exchanges before the procession went away.

" What is it? " cried the children.

Father, with hands that weren't quite steady, broke the red seals and opened the elaborate coverings. Inside was a lacquer cabinet, perhaps three feet high, richly inlaid with golden butterflies. Little double doors opened to reveal tiers of tiny drawers, each one decorated with a different design.

" It's lovely," breathed Mother. " And you deserve it too."

Everyone admired it, but it was Akio who seemed most impressed. He knelt before it a long time in silence.

" It's almost as though he were worshiping it," said Mother uneasily.

" I've seen people sit exactly like that to admire a piece of porcelain or a scroll painting," said Father. " Still they do look on the Mikado as divine. Perhaps, after all, it's better that Akio isn't going with us."

Mother nodded her head.

The next day she spoke to Father.

" Have you noticed anything different about the way we are being treated? " she asked. " People bow so very low that I feel embarrassed."

" Today," said Father, " enough runners offered to go three days' journey with us. I am to buy their rickshas then and pick up runners on the way for the rest of the journey. I have a cart, too, for the furniture."

" Is it the Mikado's cabinet? " asked Mother.

" I think so," said Father, and he laughed a little. " The Mikado's cabinet seems to be a useful as well as a beautiful gift."

# 5 . .

## The Journey

The *packing* went forward in earnest. The large pieces of furniture, the beds and the organ, were loaded on a *basha,* or two-wheeled cart, and sent ahead. Often women pulled a *basha,* a strong young girl in front and an old woman pushing in the back. But the furniture was to go a long way, and so a horse would do the pulling. When Father suggested the Mikado's cabinet should go too, O Yuki cried out that it must have a ricksha of its own.

" But, O Yuki-san," said Mother, " it is quite small and light. We couldn't afford a whole ricksha for it."

But O Yuki stood firm, and in the end the *basha* went off without the cabinet. Wrapped in the best travel cloth, it was to share the ricksha with the boys. O Yuki was satisfied. It was the next best thing to having a ricksha of its own.

" We expect to walk most of the way," said Fred. " There will be plenty of room for the cabinet."

Father smiled. " It's a long way," he said.

The last night, the family slept on the floor Japanese-fashion, and early the next morning they were ready to start on their journey. It was a beautiful day. Little white clouds floated across the bright blue sky, and the air was soft and warm, as in a chorus of good bys the line of rickshas started off.

The second day they followed a road beside the sea where fishermen were unloading their boats. Fish-filled *bashas,* many of them drawn by women, passed them on the way to market in the city. The fine large fish were spread on straw mats, the smaller fish were in tubs, and there were baskets of shining sardines.

Daisy, riding with Mother, wrinkled her nose. " Something smells bad," she said.

" It's rotting herring," said Mother. " It is to be used as fertilizer to make things grow."

After a while they came on women collecting seaweed along the beach and dumping it into steaming wooden tubs. Father had the rickshas stop for a little so that the travelers could stretch their legs and watch. The seaweed was being boiled to extract the iodine, he said.

" I know," said Ernest. " It's to put on cuts to kill germs."

" That's right," said Father.

The ricksha men rested, mopping the sweat from their faces with the blue-and-white towels they wore around their waists. Then, cheerful and uncomplaining, they started on again.

That night, they stayed at a native inn where no one had ever seen a foreigner before. The people looked at the fair-haired, blue-eyed children in astonishment, but everyone was kind and polite, and in the morning the servants gathered to call good wishes on the journey. One more day the ricksha men traveled with them, but on the third night Father paid them for their work and for the rickshas, and the men started back to their homes.

Now things went more slowly. There were no skilled runners, and Father had to go into the rice fields to hire men to draw the rickshas. They were not eager to leave their work, and they were not trained to race up and down hills as the others had done. Instead they walked, plodding along very slowly. Father and Mother too walked up most of the hills, and at first the boys joined them. But soon they were tired.

" It's all uphill," they complained.

The novelty had worn off by now, and the day seemed never-ending. When they reached an inn that night, there was no talk of staying up " just a little longer." The children were only too glad to tumble into bed, and almost at once they were asleep.

O Yuki was terribly excited. She could scarcely wait until the children were in bed before she burst out with her news.

" This is the village where I used to live," she told Mother, her voice trembling with excitement.

" But are you sure? " asked Mother. " Many villages look alike."

" I am sure," said O Yuki. " Beyond the rice fields is the house of my husband."

Mother told Father, who went to the landlord. Yes, the man remembered Kurumoto, a poor fellow, often drunk. " But I have heard nothing of him for a long time," he said.

" There was a son," said Father.

" I did not know," the man said.

" You must find him," said Mother.

Early in the morning, Father set out on his search. A raised footpath led away from the main road, and on either side stretched the wet, level rice fields. It was cold, and thin streamers of mist floated around him, almost as though he were walking in the clouds. On and on he went. It was much farther than he had expected, and the sun came up and the rice fields were steaming before he came on the charred ruins of a house.

This must be the house of O Yuki's husband, thought Father. But it was deserted. Not a soul was in sight, and he had come all the way for nothing. Then, as he stood undecided, he saw a young man coming out of a shed behind the house.

" Good morning," called Father. " Can you tell me where to find Kurumoto-san? "

The young man, who was scarcely more than a boy, looked in astonishment at this strange man with the fair skin and blue eyes. He stood quite still for a moment and then he said, " Kurumoto-san is dead."

" He had a son," said Father. " Bunji-san was his name."

" I am Bunji," said the boy.

Father looked at him. He was short but well built, with a pleasant, intelligent face.

" What was your mother's name? " asked Father.

" O Yuki-san," said the boy. " But she went away. I cannot find her, though I have tried."

" Come with me," said Father. " I will take you to her."

O Yuki had been waiting, trembling. But when she saw the strong young man, she could scarcely believe her eyes. " Is it really Bunji-san? " she faltered.

Bunji bowed low. " Most honorable Mother," he said, " I am your unworthy son. I am Bunji."

Laughing and crying by turns, O Yuki embraced him. " I never thought to see the day," she cried.

It was long past starting time, but no one disturbed them. They sat alone in the inn. O Yuki wiped her eyes with the long sleeve of her kimono and smiled.

" I am very poor," said Bunji. " I would wish to keep you with me, but I have nothing to offer, not even a roof to cover your head. My father in a drunken fit set fire to the house and died in it. There is only a shed where I sleep. The foreigners are good to you. It is better that you go with them."

" But you can come with us! " cried O Yuki. " Poate-san needs men to pull the rickshas. He will pay you."

Bunji hesitated. " But what then? " he asked. " I would have no work where you are going."

"They will need a man to work for them," said O Yuki. " Their servants would not come with them. I will ask them to take you."

One of the men had refused to go farther, and Father was glad to hire Bunji. It was partly for O Yuki's sake, of course, but soon he was glad on Bunji's account too, for the boy was cheerful and strong, and things went better because he was with them.

The next day it rained. Mother put on her mackintosh and wrapped Daisy in Father's shawl. Father and the boys put on the native capes and hats made of straw, from which the water poured in streams. The road was slippery, and they could make little headway. They were all miserable, and when they came to an inn Father decided to stop there until the next day.

In the morning it was fair, and on they went. How long was the way! It seemed it would never end. But all things do end, and on the sixth day they reached Morioka and the *daimyo*'s house. An old man with a wrinkled, kindly face stood bowing and smiling at the gate.

" This is Orikasa-san," said Father. " He is going to take care of us."

The *basha* had already come, and Orikasa had unloaded it. It was plain that he had no idea what the strange pieces of furniture were used for. The head and foot boards of a bed leaned against the organ. Only the American dresser, made by a Japanese carpenter according to Father's careful directions, but which somehow had turned into the most Japanese of cabinets, seemed to be at home.

The *daimyo*'s house was large, and the children raced through it, pushing back the sliding paper screens and peeping into built-in cupboards.

" Father! Mother! " they called. " Come look! " Their excited voices brought the others.

In a lean-to outside the house was a pile of queer-looking metal poles with sharp points.

" What are they? " asked Fred.

" They're spears," said Father.

" Please," said Orikasa. " The *samurai*, the soldiers of the *daimyo*, left them when they went away."

" May we play with them? " shouted Fred. " We can fight with them."

" Certainly not," said Father. " You'd get hurt."

" They look a little like curtain poles," said Mother.

The idea delighted Father. " That will be a good use for them," he said. " The Bible says, ' They shall beat their . . . spears into pruning hooks.' Curtain poles are next door to pruning hooks, I guess. We will help fulfill the prophecy."

After that, they walked along a garden path, unkempt but still beautiful, until they came to a tiny house, thatched with grass and with a clump of purple iris blossoming on the roof.

" A doll's house! " cried Daisy.

" It's a teahouse," said Father, " for the tea ceremony."

" But there isn't any door," said Fred, who had been exploring.

" Here," said Father, and showed them a little window-like opening with a steppingstone beneath it. " The guests took off their shoes here," he said, " and crawled through the window on their hands and knees. Let's go inside and see how things are."

He pushed aside the little sliding door, and they all crept in. There were two tiny rooms inside, separated by sliding paper doors. Leaves and cobwebs lay everywhere, but on one wall in a special place prepared for it hung a faded *kakemono,* or scroll, with a painting of peonies.

" Look what I've found," said Ernest. In a little case was a bronze teakettle with a broken handle. But its shape was charming, and on its side were Japanese characters.

Father looked at them. " ' The singing of the wind in the pines,' " he read. " That is what they call the music of the water as it boils for tea. This is something worth keeping, Ernest. We will have it mended and it can be your special treasure."

" Will this be our playhouse? " asked Daisy.

Father looked at Mother, who nodded. " Tomorrow you must clean it," she said. " It will be your very own place."

# 6..

## The Daimyo's House

Everyone *settled* down in the new home. Each day Father rode off on his bicycle to teach at the university. In the mornings Mother heard the children's lessons, and afternoons they spent at the little teahouse. There was a lot to be done there. Bunji mended the roof while Orikasa gave advice. But Mother said as the house belonged to the children they must clean the inside. They swept and dusted and were satisfied, but O Yuki shook her head.

" The woodwork must be polished by hand," she said. The boys groaned. " Must we do that? " they asked.

" Yes," said O Yuki. " The house is very well made. See, every piece of wood is well matched. There are no cracks anywhere. You must rub it with the palms of your hands to make it shine."

So the children rubbed and rubbed until the woodwork gleamed like satin. Even O Yuki was satisfied.

Orikasa, who had been hired as watchman and gardener, was really too old to do much work, so Bunji became his assistant. The men lived together in the little gatehouse. O Yuki overflowed with joy at having her son

44

with her, and Bunji was happy too. He was always good-natured and a great worker. " It would be impossible to find a better man," said Father. O Yuki's joy knew no bounds.

One day Orikasa brought a young girl to Mother. " You will like a nice girl to help with the children," he said. " She is O Hana-san."

" O Hana-san," said Mother, smiling at the little thing who bowed low before her. " ' Hana ' means ' flower.' It is a good name for you."

O Hana looked up timidly, and seeing Mother's face, she smiled too.

" How old are you, O Hana-san? " asked Mother.

" Please, I am fifteen," said O Hana.

" Will your family let you come and live with us? " Mother asked.

" I have no family," said O Hana. " My mother died long ago, and my father only lately. I have been living with relatives, but they are very poor. It is necessary that I do for myself."

So O Hana came to live in the *daimyo*'s house with the family. It was a happy day for everyone. O Hana helped O Yuki around the house, and she was a wonder with the children. She knew an endless number of stories: of ogres and foxes and ancient *samurai* warriors and the *daimyos* who used to live in their house and were gone forever. She knew games too, and her clever fingers fashioned toys of strange and ingenious make.

Every day they went for a walk, the boys drawing the express wagon with Daisy riding in it. There were many things to see. Once they came on a great boulder split wide open, and in the cleft a young peach tree was growing.

How could the rock break in half? they wondered. And how had a tree happened to grow there?

" An earthquake broke the rock," O Hana told them. " Then the soil drifted in, and at last someone dropped in a seed that took root and grew."

" I'd like to plant a seed in a hole in the rock," said Ernest. " Maybe a pine or a cherry. Let's keep our eyes open to find one."

Though they looked and looked, this was the only rock like that they ever saw. But going home that day they found the old castle. It had fallen into ruins. Weeds and moss grew in the chinks between the stones, and the lovely curving roof was falling in. Gnarled old trees surrounded it, and water lilies grew in the moat.

" Let's go in," Fred suggested.

But O Hana said: " No, it wouldn't be safe. A beam from the roof might fall, and the bridge over the moat is so old it wouldn't hold your weight." They stood and looked for a while. " The *samurai* warriors used to cross this bridge on their way to war," O Hana told them. " They wore ugly masks to scare the enemy, and their spears glistened in the sun. But that was long ago. Times are better now. Those old trees were planted when peace came to this region, so it is said."

After that they visited the castle every day. But there were other things to see. Sometimes they stopped at a little booth set up in the street to look at a flower arrangement or to watch a street vender displaying a clever mechanical toy. There always seemed to be something new for the children to discover.

Summer was passing, and now chrysanthemums bloomed everywhere. Sometimes in the morning there was frost on the ground. Then one day they woke to see everything white with snow and great white flakes swirling through the air.

The children were wild with delight. Mother said lessons could be forgotten for the day so that they could walk in the snow. Bundled against the cold, they started off in a silent world. Even the clatter of O Hana's wooden clogs was muffled by the snow. They went first to the rock. The little tree was a snowy cone on top of it.

" You'd never guess it was a tree," said Daisy.

After a while they took the road leading to the castle. Quite suddenly a snowball whizzed by them. Then another and another, and soon they were coming thick and

fast. A party of Japanese schoolboys was bearing down on them.

Fred and Ernest scooped up snow and fired away with all their might. But the enemy kept coming on.

" Foreign devils! " the schoolboys yelled. " Red-haired, green-eyed barbarians! "

" My hair is not red! " shouted Daisy angrily. And then a snowball hit her right in the face.

It was no use. They were outnumbered. " Run! " Fred gave the command. And away they went, the express cart careening from side to side, while Daisy held on for dear life. O Hana ran too. One of her clogs fell off in the snow, but she never stopped. Her little foot in its mittenlike sock went in and out of the drifts.

They burst into the house. " Take care of the women and children! " shouted Fred, and he and Ernest rushed out, spoiling for a real fight.

But when Mother came to the door, there was no one in sight. " It was only in fun," she told them. " Why don't you make a snow man before the snow melts? "

They had never seen so much snow before. Soon they had a big snowball for the body and a smaller one for the head of the snow man.

" We need some buttons to put down his front," Ernest said.

They were sticking a row of buttons into the body of the snow man when a boy slipped into the yard. Daisy was ready to run, but he called out in a friendly voice.

" Hello! My name's Kiku. Is it a Buddha you are making? "

The boys were a little shocked. " Only a snow man," they said. " Just for fun."

" Where is his face? " asked Kiku. " I'll make it." And he began working with the wet snow, adding here, taking off there. A big nose, an ugly square mouth, glaring button eyes. " Ears," said Kiku. " Big ears for wealth." It looked like one of the demons outside the gate of a temple.

One by one boys began drifting into the yard. They were friendly and smiling now.

" Let's build a fort," said Fred.

For a while they played together. Then the sun came out, and soon the snow had vanished. When they looked at the snow man his big ears had melted and water was streaming down his face. It was time for the boys to go home, but Kiku lingered for a moment.

" When will you come again? " asked Fred.

" I don't know," said Kiku. " It was a holiday today. Always we are in school."

" We study with Mother," said Daisy. " She can teach you too."

" I am the son of a *samurai*," said Kiku. " There are certain things my father expects of me." Then he went away a little sadly.

" I'm afraid he won't come again," said Fred. " His father won't let him."

⌐

It was the time for evening prayers. On the raised dais where the *daimyo* used to sit to receive his followers, Mother played the organ. The wooden shutters were pushed back, and the light shone invitingly through the paper screens. In the first weeks no one had come to prayers, but later a few, drawn by the sound of the gospel hymns and a little by curiosity, ventured in. Now there were a group of Japanese singing in their high nasal voices, their faces shining with happiness.

The children were beside the paper wall screen. Fred had been sitting Japanese-fashion with his feet under him, but his feet had gone to sleep. He changed his position, and as he did his eye caught a small wet spot on the paper screen. Someone with a wet finger was rubbing a peephole. Nudging Ernest, Fred pointed, then silently he began to crawl toward the door, Ernest close behind him. Everyone was too wrapped up in the singing to notice, and the boys gained the outdoors without being seen. Sure enough, a small figure crouched outside, busily working to make a hole in the paper wall.

Fred crept forward and pounced. " You're my prisoner," he said.

But he was not prepared for a perfect fury of flying arms and legs.

" Help! " panted Fred. " Grab him! "

Ernest had his arms, Fred his body, and together they were dragging the kicking, fighting prisoner toward the house, when they heard Daisy's voice.

" What are you *doing* to Kiku-san? " she demanded indignantly.

" Kiku-san! " exclaimed Fred, and let go so suddenly that the others almost fell over backward. " Why didn't you say you were Kiku-san? " he demanded disgustedly.

" I only wanted to see inside," sniffled Kiku.

" You needn't make a hole in our house," said Fred reasonably. " Come in. Everyone's invited."

Half reluctantly, Kiku entered with the children. The singing was over and tea was being served. Afterward Kiku and the other newcomers looked at the strange belongings of the foreigners. O Yuki did the honors, inviting them to sit in the chairs.

"Be pleased," she said, "to hang your thighs on a thigh hanger."

They admired the Swiss clock, which obligingly struck the hour, but before the Mikado's cabinet they bowed in reverence.

Kiku sat looking at it for a long time. "My ancestors served the *daimyos* for many generations," he said, "but they never received a gift from the Mikado. I will tell my father of this."

"Maybe he will come again," said Ernest after Kiku had gone.

"If he does," said Fred, "it will be because of the Mikado's cabinet."

## 7.

# Baby-san

A *new baby* had come in the night, O Yuki told the children in the morning. " A baby sister," she said, all smiles. " By and by you shall see her."

They ate breakfast by themselves. " Who wants a baby sister? " said Daisy.

" Too bad it's a girl," said Fred. " Boys are better."

Father came in rubbing his hands. " A very nice baby, if I do say so," he said. " Come and get a peep at her."

Mother was lying in bed, and beside her was a pink bundle. She lifted a corner of the blanket.

" Isn't she lovely? " Mother asked.

They looked at a red, wrinkled little face topped with a thatch of light-brown hair, and they didn't say a word.

" Take her little hand," said Mother to Daisy.

Daisy put out a cautious finger and a tiny hand closed tight around it. Suddenly she felt warm and happy.

" I'm glad we've got a baby sister," she cried.

The boys had their turn at Baby's hand then.

" Hasn't she a fine grip! " said Father proudly. " Now Mother's going to rest, and O Hana-san is ready to take you for your walk."

" On your way, stop at the gatehouse," said Mother, " and tell Orikasa-san and Bunji-san about the baby. They'll want to know."

They felt very important telling the news, and Orikasa and Bunji were properly surprised. They did not say that O Yuki had run all the way to the gatehouse to tell them early in the morning.

" I wonder what the baby's name is," said Daisy after they had started on their walk.

" Probably she hasn't got any yet," said Ernest.

" I think Plum Blossom would be nice," said Daisy.

" That's a Japanese name," Fred objected.

Daisy thought awhile. " It ought to be something that suits her," she said. " I know," and she gave a little skip. " Agrippa. Because she's got a good grip.

But the boys gave a hoot. " Herod Agrippa was a man," Fred explained. " And a very bad one. That name wouldn't do at all."

Daisy looked a little crestfallen.

" In Japan," said O Hana, " the father names the baby."

When they got home, they asked Father.

" Her name is Elizabeth," said Father.

" That's a long name for such a little baby," said Daisy. " Let's call her Baby-san."

So the baby had a pet name of her own: it was Baby-san, or Honorable Baby, and the name stayed with her for a very long time.

Orikasa and Bunji were the first ones to call on the new baby. Very clean and dressed in their best they presented themselves at the house. O Yuki brought them to the door of Mother's room, where they bowed low. They had brought gifts, which they handed to O Yuki.

" Good fortune to Honorable Baby," said Orikasa.

" Thank you, Orikasa-san and Bunji-san," said. Mother. " Baby-san thanks you too."

At that everyone laughed, and with many bows and polite drawings in of breath, Orikasa and Bunji went away.

" What's in the packages? " the children asked.

" Open them and see," said Mother.

Each package was carefully wrapped and tied with red and white paper string, and in the knot was a bit of dried fish for good luck.

They opened Orikasa's present first. Inside the paper wrapping was a box, and in the box, neatly wrapped in red paper, were two eggs.

O Yuki nodded her approval. " It is a proper gift for a baby girl," she said.

Then they opened Bunji's present. It was a tiny cloth monkey clinging to a bamboo pole, very gay with a blue head and a red body.

" O Saru! " cried O Yuki. " Honorable Monkey. Touch the spring," she directed. When they did, up flew the monkey to the top of the pole. Daisy gave a squeal of delight, and O Yuki could scarcely contain her pride. Her son had chosen his present well.

Every day people came to see the baby, for no one had ever seen a foreign baby before. They brought presents of eggs, pretty colored cloth to make her a kimono, and toys too. There was a doll with downcast eyes and a bit of gay paper for a kimono, and more Honorable Monkeys, and with every gift there was a piece of dried fish for good luck.

O Yuki was full of importance, running to and fro to greet the guests. O Hana too was busy receiving them, and in her spare time she was making a bright kimono for the baby. She took long stitches, for when it was soiled it would be ripped apart to be washed and each piece spread smoothly on a board to dry. Then it would be sewed together again. It would not be sensible to take small stitches.

It was a happy time with no lessons and always something happening. Everyone felt proud and happy because of Baby-san. Then one day there was a rude awakening.

The children were in the little teahouse when they heard some visitors talking in sad little whispers as they left after their ceremonial visit.

" Poor Poate-san, poor Poate-san," they sighed.

The children looked at each other in dismay. What was the matter? Had something gone wrong?

Then the words came clearly. " A little dragon! A little dragon with red hair and green eyes! "

A little dragon! They meant Baby-san. For a minute no one moved, then with one accord they scrambled out of the teahouse window and raced for the house.

Father saw them coming. " What's wrong? " he asked.

They told him with tears of rage. " Don't let anyone else in! " they cried. " They can't talk that way about our baby."

Father began to laugh, and Mother laughed too. " ' A haughty spirit goeth before a fall,' " quoted Father. " We were so proud, and all the time these good people were being sorry for us." And he laughed some more.

" But they called her a little dragon," said Fred, " with red hair and green eyes."

" Is her hair red and her eyes green? " asked Father.

" No! " shouted the children.

" And we know she's not a dragon," said Father. " So that's all right. What we are used to always seems best to us," he explained. " The Japanese like little Japanese children best because they're used to them. But we, of course, like our kind of babies too. That's all."

The children nodded. They could understand that, and it made them feel very much better.

One day Kiku came to call. He had come to play with

the boys once or twice since that first meeting, but this was different. They understood that, at once, when they saw the special way he was dressed. He carried a very large box, which he gave to O Yuki with a bow.

" For Baby-san," he said.

The white paper wrapping was covered with Japanese writing and tied with the usual red and white paper string, but the dried fish was folded elegantly in a piece of red paper. It was a handsome box, and inside were forty eggs, each one wrapped carefully. It was the finest gift of all.

" Stay and play," begged the children.

But Kiku, still formal and dignified, shook his head. " So sorry," he said. " Today I cannot." He started away, then turned back, his eyes sparkling. " You are to be invited to the Festival of Sons on the fifth day of the fifth month. I will tell you another time." He bowed once more and was gone.

On the seventh day after Baby-san's arrival, O Yuki cooked a dish of rice with red beans for " good fortune." Everyone ate some, and she sent portions to all the families who had paid their respects. It was important that no one be forgotten. Orikasa and Bunji were kept busy all day going from house to house with the red-bean rice. Father sent a special note of thanks to the house of Kiku. O Yuki was satisfied. All had been done properly. Baby-san was well started in life.

# 8..

## The Burglar

**O**rikasa reported that there had been burglaries in the city. He was worried for the *daimyo*'s house. Every night the heavy wooden shutters on either side of the house were closed, but Mother refused to have them fastened. She was afraid they might jam in an earthquake and keep them all prisoners in the house. Being unfastened, the shutters always rattled in an earthquake; the shutters on one side of the house would start, then as the tremor passed, those on the other side would answer them.

Orikasa did not approve of unfastened shutters.

" I am an old man," he said. " I no longer hear as in my youth, and Bunji-san sleeps the sleep of the young and healthy. A burglar might pass us without our knowing it."

He took to patrolling the grounds at night, and sometimes the light of his lantern as he made his rounds shone through the chinks of the wooden shutters.

One day he appeared at the house with a little fox terrier under his arm.

" For the children," he said. " And also," he added,

" for protection. He will be very useful."

The terrier was so little and so playful that everyone laughed at the idea of his being a protection. He capered about the room giving out little yelps, his whole body wriggling with his wagging tail.

" Here, puppy, here, puppy! " called Daisy.

" He must have a name," said Fred. " Mother, may we name him ourselves? "

" Of course. He's yours," said Mother.

There was a great argument then. " Spot " and " Towser " and " Fido " were rejected as too commonplace. The talk went on and on. Father was trying to write a letter. " What is the date? " he asked Mother above the din.

" The twenty-second of February," said Mother. " Washington's Birthday."

" That's an idea," said Fred. " Our dog came to us on Washington's Birthday. He must have a name suited to that day."

They thought of " President," " General," " Father of His Country," even " George." But none of them seemed quite right.

At last Daisy had it. " ' Cherry Tree '! " she cried.

" That's it," said Fred ." ' Cherry ' for short."

So the little Japanese dog became an American.

" Sometimes I wonder if a burglar would be any worse," sighed Mother. For Cherry was always in mischief. He chewed Father's slippers, his sharp nails scratched the matting, his wet nose made holes in the paper screens. But everyone loved him.

The children spent hours teaching him tricks. He

could sit up and beg, and roll over.

" He's smart enough to be in a circus," said Fred.

Speaking of a circus made them decide that Cherry must learn to jump through a hoop. Fred knelt with Cherry between his knees and made a circle with his arms. Ernest stood in front, holding out a biscuit.

" Jump! " Fred commanded.

But Cherry wouldn't jump. Provokingly he yawned and curled up, pretending to be asleep, though a wide-open, mischievous eye gave him away.

" Jump! " said Fred again, and prodded Cherry gently with his knee. Cherry crawled under Fred's hands and scampered away. They gave it up after a while. But the next day they cornered Cherry and tried again. This time they had him in front of the paper wall where he couldn't get away.

" Jump! " said Fred.

And Cherry jumped, a fine, clean jump that carried

him right through the paper screen.

Orikasa had to bring a man to mend the screen, and Mother said there was to be no more circus training in the house.

Each day Cherry went with the children on their walks, O Hana holding his leash, for his spirits were too high to trust him on his own. The little procession became a familiar sight, and the Japanese smiled at the children as they passed.

The days went by and nothing more was heard about burglars. The scare was almost forgotten.

" Young Matsui-san from the university wants me to speak in his village," Father told Mother.

" Of course you must," she said.

" But what about the burglar? " asked Father doubtfully. " I have to stay away all night, you know."

" It would be a brave burglar to come to a place where there are four children and four grownups, not to mention a dog," said Mother.

So it was decided that Father should go.

" I think Cherry had better sleep on my bed," suggested Fred when they were closing the shutters for the night.

" Let him sleep on my bed," said Ernest.

" I want him on my bed," said Daisy.

" I thought of it first," said Fred.

" I'll tell you," decided Mother. " Cherry will start on Fred's bed, and whoever wakes in the night and needs him may have him next."

Cherry, very happy to be allowed to stay in the house instead of being shut up in the shed, was full of tricks. It was some time before everyone could settle down, but at last all was quiet.

Fred could not tell how long he had been asleep, but he woke to find Cherry poking a cold nose in his face. One of the shutters rattled. An earthquake, he thought. But his bed felt solid beneath him and there was no answering rattle from the shutters on the opposite side of the house. Cherry made a small sound deep in his throat. Fred sat up, his hand on the little dog to quiet him.

A faint sound came to his ears. There it was again. Someone was moving in the house.

" Quiet," whispered Fred. He slipped out of bed, his hand on Cherry's collar. They crept to the doorway of the living room. It was inky dark. Fred could see nothing, but again he heard the sound of stealthy movement. His heart was pounding. He thought of Mother's story of the burglar — the man with a sword in his hand. He had killed Mr. Barker and cut off two fingers from Mrs. Barker's hand. Fred thought of Mother asleep in her bed, of Ernest and Daisy and Baby-san. He was the only one to protect them. What could he do? Burglars, he remembered, greased their bodies, so they could slip through the fingers of anyone who tried to catch them.

He won't get away from me, Fred thought. He crouched low and waited, Cherry beside him.

The room was large, and the man came slowly, cautiously feeling his way. Fred could hear his breathing. The man was almost on them. With a lunge, Fred threw himself forward and seized the man's ankles and jerked with all his might. There was a surprised grunt, a crash, and then silence. The man lay still, but Fred was taking no chances. He began to shout.

When Mother came running with a lamp, there was Fred sitting astride a man whose eyes were closed and from whose head blood was streaming down to the matting. Cherry was barking, making little rushes forward and running back.

Mother was pale, but her voice was steady. " Get up, Fred," she said. " The man is unconscious. He hit his head on the corner of the American dresser. Dear dresser! " she said suddenly. " Dear Fred," she added.

The room was full of people now. O Yuki was there and Orikasa and Bunji.

" Bunji-san, get the police," said Mother. " Orikasa-san and Fred will take charge of the prisoner."

Ernest was examining the man's wound.

" I'll get bandages," he said. " We must stop the bleeding."

In a minute he was back with a basin of water and cloths. He washed away the blood and bound up the man's head, and by the time the police came, the man was able to sit up. The police were pleased, for they had wanted the burglar for a long time. With many polite bows and many thanks, they took him away.

Now suddenly Fred was a hero. When he went out walking, people stopped to bow and congratulate him. He was Fred-san, the Honorable Fred, and if he stepped a little proudly, no wonder, with O Hana, O Yuki, Orikasa, and Bunji kowtowing to him.

" You did very well," said Father, " and we won't forget Cherry, who gave you the warning. But let's remember it was God who took care of you."

# 9..

## The Feast of Dolls

Daisy was having trouble with arithmetic. " Girls don't have to know the table of nines," she said.

" Who says they don't? " asked Mother.

" O Yuki-san," answered Daisy. " Girls are just to be good mothers. They don't need to know arithmetic."

" American girls do," said Mother. " Now try again. Nine times six — "

Reluctantly Daisy went back to her lesson, but when it was over she was as shaky as ever on the table of nines.

" I'll tell you what," said Mother. " When you know all your multiplication tables, you and I will go to the shop, and you may pick out a doll. How's that? "

Daisy's face broke into a smile. " What kind of doll? "

" Any one you like," Mother promised. " You can keep it always, a Japanese doll to have when you get to America."

It was wonderful how much easier the table of nines seemed after that! It wasn't long before Mother announced one morning that she and Daisy were going shopping.

Daisy felt very proud when they went into the shop

where the dolls were sold. A man came to meet them, bowing politely. He led them to a little raised platform where they all sat down on the floor. Then a boy brought Mother tea in a little cup without a handle. Mother put the cup on the palm of her left hand and steadied it with her right while she sipped the tea. No one was in a hurry. It was hard for Daisy to wait while the grownups talked. But after a while she began to listen.

" Soon," said the man, " it will be time for the Feast of Dolls, the third day of the third month. Then for three days the dolls which have been in the family for years will be brought out and displayed for everyone to see.

" I, and my humble family before me," he went on, " have had the honor of making all the dolls for the house of the Baron Hidegawa. In their fireproof warehouse are dolls dating back three hundred years, all made by members of my family."

" How wonderful! " said Mother. " Are these dolls of any special kind? "

" There must always be a doll emperor and empress," said the man, " and five court musicians. The others are not so important. From time to time, new groups of royal dolls are added. In the Hidegawa collection there are many emperor and empress dolls, belonging to different periods in the family history. This year a new group is to be added. We are making them now. Would you care to see them? "

" Oh, please. We would like that! " cried Mother, her cheeks quite pink with pleasure.

The man turned to give an order, and soon a boy came carrying the dolls. Their costumes were made of brocade, stiff with gold, their skirts flaring in wide folds.

" The emperor and empress," said the man proudly.

" Do little girls play with them? " asked Daisy.

" No," said the man. " But each day of the feast they bring food to the dolls. It is served in special dolls' dishes." He turned to the boy again, and soon tiny Satsuma bowls were being placed before the dolls. " For rice," said the man.

" Oh! Oh! " cried Daisy. And no wonder, for the rice bowls were so tiny they seemed like fairy bowls.

After they had been properly admired, the man turned to Daisy. " Perhaps the honorable little girl is to have a doll," he said.

" Yes," said Daisy shyly. " I know my multiplication tables, so I have earned one."

Again the boy was sent on an errand, and this time he came back with his arms full of dolls dressed in as many bright colors as a garden of flowers.

" I'm afraid it will be hard to choose from all these," said Mother.

But Daisy had already chosen in her own mind. It was a doll with straight black hair and bright black eyes, and her kimono was covered with pink cherry blossoms. Daisy could see nothing half so nice, and the sale was soon made.

Then Mother and the man and Daisy and the boy all bowed to each other. Daisy, hugging the new doll, had turned to leave the shop when suddenly a chorus of shouts made her run to Mother in alarm.

" It's all right," Mother reassured her. " They're only saying thank you and come again."

" But they make so much noise," said Daisy, looking

timidly at the employees and customers who had all gathered to say good-by. Even after Mother and Daisy had reached the street, the shouted thanks followed them. It was strange to hear so much noise coming from people who were usually so quiet.

" I'm going to call my new doll ' O Yuki,' " said Daisy. " She will be company for Kate. Japanese and American dolls should be good friends."

It was the end of the second month, and the family were gathered for breakfast when O Yuki hurried into the room.

" Please, Poate-san," she began, her voice trembling with excitement, " there is a messenger from the Baron Hidegawa to see you."

Father looked up in surprise. " The Baron Hidegawa," he repeated. " Now what can he want with me? " He got up quickly and started for the door.

" May I come too? " asked Fred.

" No," said Father firmly. " You stay right here." Then he was gone.

The children tried to peek around the sliding door, but it was no use. There was no one in sight. It seemed a long time before Father came back. He had a letter stamped all over with sealing wax.

" It's an invitation, my dear," he said to Mother. " You and Daisy are invited to the Feast of Dolls at the house of the Baron Hidegawa."

Mother was astonished. " A foreigner to be asked there! " she said.

" It is strange," said Father. " I understand the Baron

is of the old school and hates all the new ways. The Baroness is very young, and he never allows her to go anywhere. I can't understand how the Baron came to invite you."

" It's because of the Mikado's cabinet," Fred spoke up.

Father thought a moment. " You may be right," he said.

" But aren't you invited? " asked Mother.

" No, indeed," said Father. " The Feast of Dolls is not for mere men. The boys and I will stay at home that day."

" But how can Daisy and I go alone? " wailed Mother. " And what can I wear? "

" Your very best," said Father.

" My best? " Mother laughed. " I suppose I could wear my wedding dress," she said doubtfully. " And isn't it lucky," she added, brightening, " it's still cool enough for Daisy to wear the blue velvet coat and bonnet Aunt Adelaide sent from New York? Daisy," she said, " you must be very polite. Dear me," she laughed, " I believe I'm excited."

" It isn't every foreigner who gains admittance to the house of a baron of the old school," said Father. " Daisy, you must watch everything very carefully. It will be something to tell your grandchildren about."

On the third day of the third month, Bunji, in new clothes and with a handsome monogram on the back of his kimono, took Mother and Daisy in a ricksha to the house of the Baron Hidegawa. Mother's cheeks were pink with excitement. She looked very pretty in the wedding dress of gray silk with its many pleated ruffles. Daisy's blue velvet matched the color of her eyes.

" I'm proud of you both," said Father, as the whole household came out to wave good-by.

" Please wait here, Bunji-san," said Mother when they reached the great gates gleaming in gold and lacquer. A little timidly she took Daisy's hand and went past the bowing gatekeeper into the private grounds of the Baron.

It was beautifully green and quiet. A tiny waterfall played into a pool. A stone lantern stood beside the path, and that was all they saw before two little girls in bright kimonos appeared for a moment in a doorway. The girls ran away as soon as they caught sight of the visitors, and a lady in waiting bowed low, inviting them to enter. They took off their shoes in a little anteroom and felt the matting deep and soft beneath their feet. Then they entered a long, low room, bare except for the mats and a few cushions on the floor. But the light filtering through the paper walls cast a mellow glow, the woodwork gleamed from much polishing, and on the sliding doors was a painting of cherry blossoms and pheasants.

The Baroness Hidegawa was tiny and pretty. In her kimono, embroidered with cherry blossoms, she seemed scarcely older than the little girls. She bowed low, and so did Mother. The two little girls knelt, their heads almost touching the floor. Mother looked quickly at Daisy. She too was kneeling, the ruffle of her bonnet just clearing the matting. O Hana had taught her well.

They sat on the floor and made conversation while tea was served. The Baroness after a few timid minutes was eager to hear about their lives.

" You have two sons. You are fortunate indeed," she sighed.

The girls nibbled sweetmeats and waited; only their sparkling eyes showed their excitement. At last the ceremony of tea was over, and they were free to go on to the next room.

Such a sight as met their eyes! Long, red-covered shelves, tier on tier, stretched the length of the room, and on the shelves were ranged hundreds of dolls with all their tiny belongings. On the top shelf sat the royal dolls,

beginning with the oldest emperor and empress and going on to the latest, which Daisy recognized as the ones she had seen in the shop. Each royal couple sat above its five court musicians with their musical instruments, and before each was an elegant tea service with tiny trays, plates, and cups. There were palanquins too and lacquered bullock carts with bowlegged black bulls to draw them. And everything was tiny and perfect and made exactly to scale.

"Tami-san and Sada-san," said the Baroness, "show the honorable little one everything she wishes to see."

The girls moved slowly along, gazing at each tiny, perfect treasure.

"It is time now to feed the dolls," said Tami, at last.

So Sada and Daisy put grains of rice into all the rice bowls, and Tami, who was older and very clever, filled the little cups with tea without spilling a drop.

It was a day of enchantment, but at last the time to leave had come.

"Be pleased to come again," said Tami and Sada.

"I long for your return," said the Baroness.

They all bowed low. As Mother and Daisy went down the path, the sweet voices of the children followed them. "*Sayonara*," they called. "*Sayonara*. Good-by."

# 10..

## The Festival of Sons

Bunji was sitting in the kitchen with O Yuki. She could never get used to the joy of having her son again, and Bunji was very good to her. He never seemed to mind how many times she asked him, " Do you remember? " He was full of good spirits, and often there was laughter in the kitchen. They were not alone. O Hana was there too, sitting quietly, not often speaking, but not missing a word that was said. And often Bunji's eyes turned to where she was sitting, as though much that he said was meant for her.

Ernest came into the room with Father's big doctor book under his arm. " I'm studying the human frame," he said. He put the book down on the floor and opened it to the picture of a man with bulging muscles. " Bunji-san," he said, " will you please clench your fist and then bend your elbow. I want to feel your biceps."

Always obliging, Bunji bent his elbow. As the muscles swelled on his upper arm, Ernest watched in admiration. " Splendid! " he said.

" What is splendid? " asked O Yuki, anxious to know anything in which her Bunji excelled.

" His biceps," said Ernest. " The muscles that move his arm. Bunji-san's swell like anything."

He turned to study the book again, then felt Bunji's legs. " He has fine leg muscles too," he decided. " That's because he is a great worker."

Bunji was pleased. " Your head is better than my unworthy muscles," he said. " Poate-san is lucky to have two fine sons."

" Yes," said O Yuki, " they are brave and good. Ernest-san is also kind. He bound up the wounds of the burglar who cut his head on the American dresser. Ernest-san is kind even to an enemy."

It was Ernest's turn to be pleased; his face turned red at such praise.

" Has Poate-san provided the fish for the Festival of Sons? " asked Bunji.

" When is it? " asked Ernest.

" On the fifth day of the fifth month comes the Festival of Sons," said Bunji. " Then in front of every house blessed with boys, paper carp will hang on poles for all to see."

" Why carp? " asked Ernest.

" Because," said Bunji, " carp are very strong fish. They swim up the mountain streams against the current. They are brave and strong as boys must be."

That night, Ernest asked about the Festival of Sons. " May we buy some paper carp to hang in front of our house? "

" What do you think? " Father turned to Mother.

" Why shouldn't we let everyone know that we have two sons? " she asked. " We are proud of them."

So the next day when they went for their walk, O Hana took them to a shop that sold paper carp. The shop was only an open booth with curtains of dark blue covered with Japanese writing. But there were hundreds of paper fish, some tied to poles and swinging in the breeze, others in piles on the shelves. They were made double with wide-open mouths so that the wind could blow in and fill the bodies. As they bobbed high in the air on the tops of the poles, they looked strangely lifelike. Fred chose a very large fish of black and gold, and Ernest, as the younger brother, one a little smaller with blue and green markings and round, staring, red eyes.

They took their fish home proudly, and on the fifth day of the fifth month Orikasa produced a tall bamboo pole and fastened the fish, one above the other, on the end of it, and Bunji drove the pole into the ground beside the house. At first the fish hung limp, then as a breeze stirred they billowed out, and soon they were leaping and tossing on their poles, as though they were fighting their way upstream against the current.

" Carp is for boy," said Orikasa. " Boy must be strong and brave."

Long ago Kiku had said that the boys would be invited to his house for the Festival of Sons, and he did not forget. A letter stamped with many red seals came from Kiku's father inviting them. Bunji went with them to Kiku's house, for it would not be proper for O Hana to go to a boys' festival.

As they went along the streets, they saw before almost every house gay paper fish bobbing and swinging on their poles. The boys counted them as they passed.

" Three boys in this house," said Ernest. " Four in the one next door."

" If Daisy and Baby-san were only boys," said Fred, " we could have four carp too."

Kiku lived in a fine, large house surrounded by a high wall. Only one fish flew on the pole beside the gate, though that one was big and handsome. Kiku met them with bows of ceremony.

" You have a very fine paper carp," said Fred politely.

" Only one," said Kiku. " I am the only son. All the other children are girls. A great misfortune."

"We like our girls," said Fred quickly. Quite suddenly he knew he wouldn't trade Daisy and Baby-san for any number of boys.

Kiku took them into the house to see the display set out especially for the festival. On red-covered shelves were pictures of national heroes, warriors in armor, some with hideous masks to frighten the enemy. There were suits of armor too, belonging to *samurai* ancestors, and spears, and a sword that Kiku said had been in the family for hundreds of years. The flowers in the niche of honor were iris, because their "leaves are like swords," Kiku explained.

"Say, this is great," said Fred.

"It's very warlike," said Ernest.

"Of course," said Kiku. "War has always been the business of the *samurai*. But times have changed," he sighed. "There are no more wars. My father, instead of being a warrior, must be a merchant of tea. I also must follow in his steps. It is necessary that we Japanese learn the ways of the outside world. Therefore I must learn English. Perhaps I shall go to school in America."

"We are going to America in another year," said Fred. "I have to go to school too."

"Perhaps we shall meet," said Kiku.

He broke off as a Japanese gentleman came quietly into the room. "My father," said Kiku, and bowed. "Fred-san and Ernest-san, the sons of the foreigner who has a cabinet, the gift of the Emperor."

Kiku's father bowed, and the boys bowed too. They felt very uncomfortable in the presence of this man, who was not at all like Bunji and Orikasa. He was very formal. His kimono was of the richest silk, and in his sash were two swords, one large and one small.

"Your honorable father teaches English at the university?" asked Kiku's father. Even his voice was different, so that his speech seemed unfamiliar.

"Yes, sir," said Fred.

"Perhaps," said Kiku's father, "he would condescend to instruct my son. I will do myself the honor to wait upon him." Then he bowed and left the room.

For a minute no one said anything. It seemed that he had left something stiff and forbidding behind him. Fred cleared his throat.

" Why does he have two swords? " he asked in a low voice.

" All *samurai* have two swords," said Kiku. After a pause, he went on, " My father doesn't wear the swords in these times except on such a day as this when we recall the warlike past."

Soon refreshments were served, a kind of rice dumpling wrapped in oak leaves, " because," said Kiku, " like the carp, the oak tree stands for courage. Boys must be strong and brave."

Kiku's father did not come back, but the boys were afraid he might. They were glad when it was time to go home.

" Did you have a good time? " asked Father.

" Not very," said Fred.

" What's that verse about swords and curtain poles? " asked Ernest.

" ' They shall beat their swords into plowshares, and their spears into pruning hooks,' " quoted Father.

" I wish they would," said Ernest.

Father had a visitor a few days later. " Kiku's father has asked me to tutor the boy in English," he told Mother.

" You are going to do it? " asked Mother.

" Yes," said Father. " Kiku is to come here for his lessons. Nothing was said about payment. That, of course, wouldn't be etiquette. When the boy comes he will bring the proper present with him. Not that I wouldn't be glad to teach him for nothing, but the pride of a *samurai* would not permit that. How I hope that, along with the English, I can teach him a little love and kindness! "

# 11..

## O Hana and Bunji

Come, Cherry, jump!" coaxed Fred. "Good dog. Jump!" But Cherry was in no mood to jump. He yawned and lay down, one eye cocked for mischief.

"Cherry!" shouted Kiku, losing his temper. He drew back his foot for a kick, but Fred was too quick for him.

"Look out!" he said, and gave Kiku a shove.

"What did you do that for?" demanded Kiku fiercely.

"No one's going to kick my dog," said Fred just as fiercely.

"Why not, if he doesn't obey?" demanded Kiku.

"Because it's no way to treat a dumb animal that can't stand up for himself. That's why," said Fred.

Kiku had had his English lesson, and now at Father's suggestion he was spending an hour with the boys to practice what he had learned. In the heat of their discussion they had forgotten and were talking in Japanese. Now Fred went back to English.

"You don't say 'Cherry' right," he said. "It's Cher-ry."

Kiku didn't say anything. He only looked sulky.

"Never mind," said Ernest. "Cherry's part Japanese.

Maybe he doesn't say his name our way either."

At that they all laughed and the quarrel was forgotten.

Kiku had brought a fine red hoop and they had been trying, outdoors this time, to coax Cherry to jump through it. Now they gave up and sat down on the path to rest. Bunji was coming toward them with a bundle of firewood on his back. Fred and Ernest scrambled out of his way, but Kiku did not move, and Bunji went around him.

" You're funny," said Kiku. " You stick up for a dog and get out of the way of a servant. And your father walks beside your mother on the street. A Japanese man would never do that."

Fred thought a moment. " It's only being kind," he said. " It's part of the Golden Rule, I guess."

" What is the Golden Rule? " asked Kiku.

" ' Do unto others as you would have them do to you,' " said Fred.

Kiku stared. He had never heard of such a thing. After that, they talked of other things, but when Kiku went away, he stooped to give Cherry a pat. Perhaps Fred's words had more effect than he knew.

Orikasa, in a clean kimono and with an air of great importance, presented himself at the house.

Mother was singing to Baby-san. " Come in," she invited.

" Please," said Orikasa, " I would like to speak to Poate-san on a certain matter."

Father was in his study and invited Orikasa to come in. He pushed the sliding doors shut and he and Orikasa talked together. After a while Father called Mother, and then O Hana. When O Hana left the study, she held the big sleeve of her kimono to her eyes. She was trembling and her color came and went, first pink, then white. She ran away to her room without looking at the children.

" What is it? " they wanted to know.

" It's a secret," said Mother. " Don't tease O Hana to tell you."

O Hana did not wait on table that night, and she

missed evening prayers. There seemed to be a coolness between her and O Yuki after that, and when Bunji came into the kitchen, O Hana did not sit with them. Ernest found it was no longer fun to go to the kitchen with his doctor book. O Hana was not there, and Bunji had nothing to say for himself.

Things might have gone on that way indefinitely if Father hadn't caught a bad cold. He came back from the university, his eyes streaming and his voice a mere croak.

" I ache all over," he said dismally.

Mother put him to bed with a hot drink and the little hand warmer to keep him warm.

" What about prayers? " he asked. He couldn't bear to think of there being no evening prayers.

" We can sing hymns, you know," said Mother.

Afterward she talked to the children. " I wish we could have the call to prayer," she said. " I don't want people to stay away because they don't hear it."

" I could give it," said Fred. " Only," he added, " I suppose it needs a man. What about Orikasa-san? "

" He is so old," said Mother. " His voice is too thin and reedy. I could do better myself, only it would never do for a woman to give the call to prayer."

" Bunji-san could do it," said Ernest, eagerly putting forward his favorite.

" He goes to the Shinto temple," said Mother.

" Not for a long time," said Ernest.

But Mother shook her head. " I'll start to play the organ early," she decided. " People can hear that, anyway."

When the time came, they lighted the student lamp

and put it where it shone invitingly through the paper
walls. Mother started toward the organ, then they all
stood still, listening. From somewhere outdoors came a
man's voice, strong and clear, raised in the call to prayer.

" It's Bunji-san! " cried Ernest.

Bunji was coming up the path. Once more he stopped
and repeated the call before entering the house. People

were following him, shyly and politely, as they always did. The little service began. They sang and sang, and Bunji, who had always sat silent, joined in the hymns. He and Mother carried everyone along with music such as they had never heard before. O Hana watched with shining eyes.

"Oh, Bunji-san," said Mother, when everyone had gone, "how can I ever thank you?"

Bunji sucked in his breath with pleasure. "Please," he said, "do not thank me. I have lived a long time in this family. Before, my life was most miserable. Now it is most happy. I am your servant and I want to be the servant of your Lord."

The next day Father was much better. He and Mother were sitting in the study when loud voices were heard in the kitchen. Mother went to see what was the matter. O Yuki was talking excitedly to Orikasa.

"Please, I have a little word to say to Poate-san," said Orikasa when he saw Mother.

They left O Yuki nodding and smiling and went into the study. Father listened to what Orikasa had to say, then he sent for O Hana. At last, he went to the door and called, "Bunji-san."

Strange to say, Bunji was right there to answer.

"Bunji-san," said Father, "Orikasa-san has told me that you want O Hana-san for your wife. Is that so?"

"Please, yes," said Bunji, and bowed very low.

"Now that you are a Christian, O Hana-san is willing. O Hana-san is a lovely girl and you are a good man. We think you will be happy together. God bless you."

So it was decided that O Hana and Bunji would be

married. O Yuki's joy knew no bounds. Her son was a Christian, and he was to marry O Hana, the girl she loved with all her heart. She went about her work singing.

Now a time of happiness descended on them all. The children's lessons went well. Kiku studied hard, and his English improved. He spent much time at Poate-san's house, and his father did not object, because it was good for his English.

" To the *samurai,* war and knowledge are like the two wings of a bird," said Kiku's father.

Orikasa sat in the sun warming himself. But Bunji redoubled his work about the place. The iris bloomed on the little teahouse roof, and when the chrysanthemums flowered, O Hana and Bunji would be married and live in the gatehouse to take care of Orikasa in his old age. O Yuki too would be safe with them.

" When we go to America, they will all be together," said Mother, and sighed. She was half glad, half sorry at the thought of going.

# 12..

## The Walking Trip

It's spring," said Father. " Everybody in Japan will soon be starting off on a walking trip."

" Why can't we go too? " asked Fred.

For a minute no one said anything, then Mother nodded her head. " You could go, you know," she said to Father. " You have vacation next week, and you and the boys could take a trip together to the Hot Springs."

" Do you think the boys are big enough? " asked Father.

" Big enough! " cried Fred. " I'm as tall as Bunji-san."

" And I'm pretty near as tall," said Ernest, standing very straight.

Mother looked at her boys. " I think they could walk to the Hot Springs all right," she said. " They ought to have a taste of mountain climbing before we leave Japan."

" Hurray! We're going to the Hot Springs! " shouted the boys excitedly.

" I want to go too," cried Daisy.

" You're too little," said Fred.

" I am not," said Daisy. " I can walk like anything."

86

" I'll need you here to help take care of Baby-san," said Mother.

" O Hana-san can take care of Baby-san," said Daisy.

" Mother isn't going with us," Father pointed out. " This trip is for men only. But I tell you what. Later in the summer we'll have a family holiday and you can help plan it. How's that? "

" Wel-l," said Daisy a little unwillingly. Then she clapped her hands. " I've thought of a place," she said. " Only I won't tell you yet."

" What will we take with us on our travels? " asked Fred. " Will I need my second-best suit? "

" No, no," said Father.

" Our night clothes? " said Ernest.

" No," said Father again. " The inns will give us clean cotton kimonos to sleep in. All we'll need will be soap and a toothbrush and handkerchiefs. On a walking trip, he who travels lightest travels best."

" I'll take my compass," Fred decided. " It will come in handy if we get lost." His eyes sparkled at such a fine idea.

" I'll take my magnet," said Ernest. " There are probably minerals in the mountains and I can do some prospecting."

Of course they told Kiku. " You are very lucky," he said. " I have never been on a pilgrimage," he added a little wistfully.

Fred and Ernest looked at each other, and the very same thought popped into both their heads. But they didn't say anything then. That night they talked to Father.

" Could Kiku go too? " they asked. " We would be careful not to eat very much and then we could share with him. Please, Father."

" I don't think it will be necessary for you to go without eating," said Father. " If Kiku's father is willing, I think it would be a fine plan for him to go along."

" Three boys! " Mother laughed. " I wonder if you realize what you're getting into."

" I don't think we'll have any trouble," said Father easily.

" We'll always do exactly as we're told," said Fred.

" We'll be very good," said Ernest.

Kiku's father was willing, and in the next few days the

boys walked on air. Everyone was up early on the day they were to start. The boys were ready, each one with a small bundle slung over his shoulder. Father, besides his bundle, had an alpenstock which he had brought back from a vacation in Switzerland long ago. It had a curved handle and on the other end a sharp iron spike which could be driven into the ground to help on steep places in the climb.

The whole household went as far as the gatehouse to see them off. Orikasa, O Yuki, O Hana, and Bunji bowed low to say good-by, and Daisy and Mother with Baby-san in her arms waved their hands. Cherry was there, of course, ready to go along.

" Stay there," said Fred sternly.

" Have a good time," said Mother, and the travelers started. But Cherry went bounding after them.

" Go home," said Fred. But Cherry had no intention of going home. He had to be dragged back to the gate-house so that Daisy could hold him. " Good-by, good-by," everyone called. The travelers were on their way.

There were plenty of others on the road. Some, like themselves, were walking for pleasure, but many wore the white clothes of pilgrims and were on their way to visit the shrines of national heroes. Under the broad-brimmed pilgrim hats were wrinkled, old faces, as well as young ones. But young and old were as happy as children on a picnic.

Mother had put up a lunch, and Father and the boys sat down beside the road to eat. " Here's a big crowd coming," said Fred, as a number of white-clad pilgrims

came into sight. Two of them were carrying a banner, and
another, the leader, walked ahead, pointing out the things
he thought they ought to look at.

" It's a pilgrim society," said Kiku. " They have saved
for a whole year, one penny a month. Then at the end of
the year they drew lots to see who would be the lucky
ones to go on the pilgrimage."

The pilgrims as they passed smiled and bowed to Father and the boys. " Do you go to the Hot Springs? " they
called. " We will see you there."

" They sleep outdoors," said Kiku, " and cook their
meals over a little fire. They are very poor, but, as you
see, very happy."

After a while Father stood up and the boys, a little unwillingly, followed.

" It's very hot," said Fred.

" My feet hurt," said Ernest.

Kiku didn't say anything, but he was not as cheerful as
when they started.

" See how much closer the mountains are than they

were this morning," Father said encouragingly.

" They look pretty far away to me," said Fred wearily.

" You've done very well for the first day," Father said.
" The very next likely-looking inn we come to, we'll stop
and spend the night."

It was a strange thing. They had passed many inns dur-
ing the day, but now that they wanted one there seemed
none to be found.

" How much longer do we have to go? " groaned Ernest.

" There's one! " cried Fred at last.

It was a big place, finer than any the boys had ever seen.
" Do you think we can afford to stay here? " asked Ernest
uneasily.

" I'm sure we can," Father reassured him, and turned in at the gate.

" Welcome! Welcome! " shouted the landlord, as he and all his servants came running to greet the guests. Menservants brought hot water to the veranda, and Father and the boys took off their shoes and stockings and washed their feet before going in.

" How nice and cool it is in here," said Fred, looking around the clean inn with its pretty, enclosed garden.

" It's good to sit down," sighed Ernest.

" That's what I say too," said Father, as they sank down on cushions spread on the floor. A maid brought them tea.

" O, thank you," they cried gratefully.

She bowed to Father. " The water is ready for the honorable one's bath," she said.

Father turned to the boys. " It takes a long time for the bath water to heat," he explained. " And it's hard to empty the tub, so we will all have to take a bath in the same water. Kiku is our guest. Perhaps he should have the first bath."

Kiku was shocked at such an idea. " Poate-san," he said, " I am too insignificant for this honor. I beg that you will bathe first."

" Let's go according to ages," said Ernest. " I don't mind being last." For Ernest didn't like baths very much anyway.

" That's a good plan," said Father, and followed the maid down the hall to the bathroom. It was Fred's turn next. There was a basin of water on a bench in the bathroom, and he washed himself first, Japanese-fashion, before getting into the tub. The water was so deep that it

came right up to his chin. It was very hot too, and no
wonder, for there was a charcoal fire burning under it.
It was so pleasant that he hated to climb out and put on
the clean kimono the maid had left him.

By the time everyone had had a bath, supper was ready.
The maids brought it on low tables which they set before
the guests, and knelt to serve them.

" This is something *like*," whispered Ernest.

But Fred gave him a nudge. No need to let people
know they weren't used to such luxury.

" These shellfish are very good," said Father. " Have
some, boys."

But Kiku shook his head. " Sometimes honorable shellfish cause sickness of the stomach," he said.

" Oh, I think these are all right," said Father.

All the same Kiku and Fred decided not to eat any.
" All the more for us," said Ernest, nodding to Father,
and they cleared the dish.

By the time the meal was over, the boys could scarcely
keep their eyes open. So at Father's word, the maids slid
paper screens into grooves in the floor, and all at once
they were shut in a snug little room of their own.

The maids brought out four mattresses and spread
them in a row on the floor, then they added the covers
and the hard Japanese pillows.

" One, two, three," counted Father, " into bed you go."
And almost before he had finished counting, the boys had
dived beneath the covers. Soon everyone was fast asleep.

" Father, Father, I'm dreadfully sick."

Father was having a bad dream, but he woke at the

sound of Ernest's voice. "Coming," he mumbled, but when he tried to get up, the whole world seemed to fall down on him. There was a roaring in his ears and he was deathly sick. He remembered what Kiku had said about shellfish. If only he had listened!

Maids came running with basins and water. The landlord stood bowing in the doorway. "So sorry," he kept saying. "Sugar is the cure for this sickness."

"Oh, I couldn't," shuddered Father. He took one spoonful the maid offered and that was all he could manage. He could hear Ernest crunching away, and his stomach turned over. Time went on and things got better. Through it all, Fred and Kiku slept soundly. At last, full of sugar, Ernest dropped off, but Father felt no better. The hard Japanese pillow hurt his head, but he didn't dare move for fear of being sick again. It was morning before he slept.

When he opened his eyes, a maid was kneeling beside him with a bowl full of sugar on a tray. "The honorable one must eat sugar to get well," she said.

Obediently Father took the bowl and swallowed a spoonful of sugar. "Where are the boys?" he asked weakly.

"They have gone to the *Tengu*'s Wind Hole," said the maid.

"But the sick boy," said Father, trying to struggle to his feet.

"He is quite well," the maid assured him. "He ate all the sugar."

So, grimly, Father finished the bowl of sugar. Then he lay down and quite suddenly he was asleep.

# 13..

## The Tengu's Wind Hole

**K**iku and Fred woke in fine spirits, but before they could say a word a maid appeared in the doorway with a finger on her lip.

" The honorable father was sick in the night," she whispered. " Do not wake him."

" It was the shellfish," said Kiku wisely.

" And how is the honorable younger brother? " asked the maid, turning to Ernest.

Were you sick too? " asked Fred curiously.

" Some," said Ernest. He didn't want to admit how awful it had been. " I'm all right now," he added. And to his surprise, it seemed to be true.

The boys dressed quietly and slipped out without disturbing Father. Ernest didn't feel much like eating breakfast. He sipped some tea and ate a little rice. But no one seemed to notice.

" What will we do today? " Fred asked. " If Father's sick, we ought to have a plan of our own."

" You could go to the *Tengu's* Wind Hole," suggested the landlord, who had been hovering about. " It is not far away."

" How do we get there? " asked Fred.

" The road runs beside the river gorge," said the land-lord, pointing. " Follow it until you come to the Tea-house of the Hanging Rocks. The old couple who keep the place will tell you how to go from there."

" ' The *Tengu*'s Wind Hole,' " repeated Fred. " That's an odd name. What is a *tengu*? "

The landlord looked quickly about. " It is not well to ask such questions," he said, and hurried away.

" Now, what's the matter with him? " asked Fred of Kiku. " Do you know what a *tengu* is? "

" It is a spirit who lives in lonely places," said Kiku. " Sometimes it is unfriendly." And that was all he would say.

" Well," said Fred, " we can just have a look at his wind hole, I guess."

" Do you think we ought to go without asking Father? " Ernest wondered. He didn't feel much like going anywhere.

" Why not? " asked Fred. But he tiptoed down the hall to have a look at Father. " He's asleep," he reported. " It's much better for him to be left alone. I have my compass. We can chart our course by it. It will be more scientific."

So they started off. The road was narrow and steep, running along the top of a deep, rocky gorge. They could see the river far below, churning and foaming over great boulders.

" See those rocks," said Kiku. " They fell down from up here. Every little while there has been a landslide. You can tell by looking at the side of the ravine."

Fred was fascinated, but Ernest didn't like the black rocks and the angry river. It was a lonely place, bare and desolate, with only a few stunted pines clinging to the cliff. They started up the path, Kiku, quick and sure-footed, in the lead and Fred close behind.

"Don't go so fast," called Ernest. But the boys didn't hear him. He was soon left far behind.

He didn't feel well. His head ached and his knees were shaky, and the farther he went the worse he felt. Once he stumbled, and the horrid thought came to him that he might fall over the edge into the river. After that he kept his eyes on the ground and never looked to right or left. The path twisted and turned around great boulders, and then he came to a place that seemed to go straight up.

He put an uncertain foot on a big stone and, reaching up, caught hold of the branch of a pine tree that overhung the gorge. He was going to pull himself up by it, when suddenly the stone under his foot turned over, and the whole bank gave way. For a second he clung there, his feet dangling over the edge. He heard the sound of falling stones and dirt and a splash as the landslide struck the water. The pine tree trembled but stood its ground, and, scrambling and clawing, Ernest worked his way to safety. There he lay, not daring to look up to see what had happened.

"Ernest!" Fred was shouting. "Ernest, are you all right?" Fred and Kiku came dashing down the path. "We heard the avalanche. We came as fast as we could," panted Fred.

Ernest didn't move. "I can't go on," he said. "You'll have to leave me here."

" I'll never leave you! " cried Fred, and flung himself down beside his brother.

It was Kiku who thought of what to do. " The teahouse can't be far away," he said. " We can help Ernest-san to get there, and he can lie down and have something to eat. You know you didn't eat much breakfast," he said to Ernest.

He spoke so sensibly that Ernest began to feel better. He even tried to sit up. At first, everything seemed to spin round and round, but after a minute things righted themselves, and he got to his feet. There was a great hole where the path had been, and when he saw it, he felt sick all over again.

" Lean on me," said Fred, and put an arm around him. Kiku took his other arm and they began to climb.

Almost at once they saw the teahouse perched on the very edge of the rocks overhanging the river. A little old woman, with her kimono tucked up over tight blue cotton pants, came running to meet them.

"Good grandmother," said Kiku, "the young foreigner is sick, as you can see."

The old woman knew just what to do. She spread a mattress on the floor for Ernest to lie down on, and then she brought them tea.

"Thank you," said Ernest, and drank it eagerly, remembering to make smacking noises as Orikasa did, for politeness.

Kiku put a coin on the tea tray. "*Chadai*," he said. "Tea money. Good grandmother, we are hungry. Please give us something to eat."

She bowed her thanks. "I will prepare food for the honorable young sirs," she said. "Be pleased to enter the poor shop of my husband while you wait." She slid back the paper partition to show a tiny workshop where an old man sat carving on a queer shaped root. Fred and Kiku went in and the old woman returned to where Ernest was lying.

"I have a very powerful medicine," she said, taking a bottle out of a cupboard. "It is a snake pickled in rice wine. It will make you well." She gave the bottle a shake, and the snake inside writhed in a very lifelike way.

Ernest had to shut his eyes for a minute. "Honorable grandmother," he said, "I am not worthy to take this honorable medicine. I pray you keep it for yourself and your venerable husband."

The old woman hesitated. "Are you sure you don't need it?" she asked.

" I am sure," said Ernest, and sat up straight to prove it.

Smiling with relief, the old woman put her precious medicine back into the cupboard and went about preparing food.

Kiku and Fred were admiring the strange birds and beasts the old man had carved from gnarled roots. They made Fred think of the paintbrush holder at home with the face of an old man, but these carvings were much better.

Kiku was looking at a sort of goblin with a hideous beaked nose. " It is a *tengu*," he said to Fred.

" He doesn't look very friendly," said Fred.

" Hush! " said Kiku quickly. " How much? " he asked, turning to the old man.

The old man named a price, but Kiku shook his head. " Too much," he said.

When the old man lowered the price, Kiku still shook his head. So they argued and haggled, to Fred's amazement, until a bargain was struck. Then with smiles and bows Kiku paid his money and the *tengu* was his.

Now their meal was ready, and they sat on the floor, looking out over the river, and ate rice and bean marmalade. Perhaps the very thought of the snake medicine had cured Ernest. At any rate he sat up and ate as much as anybody.

" Where is the *Tengu*'s Wind Hole? " asked Fred when it was time to go.

The old couple went to the door and pointed. " See that pile of rocks," said the old man. " It is there. Long ago the *tengu* built it. There were many of them in those days, but only one *tengu* is left. He sits in the hole at the bottom of the rocks, and his breath blows cold even in the summer."

" Have you ever seen him? " asked Kiku.

" No," said the old man. " But he guides my hand when I carve his face."

" We have never seen the *tengu*," said the old woman, " but often we see the big snake, the messenger of the god of the mountain. He lies in the sun or crosses the path near the wind hole."

The boys said good-by and started off in the direction of the wind hole. After a minute, Fred stopped and took his compass out of his pocket. " We'd better take our bearings," he said. " West by south," he said. " That means when we go back, we must go east by north. Just as well to know where we stand." He pocketed his compass again.

As they came nearer to the pile of rocks, it seemed to grow bigger and more forbidding.

" The *tengu* who built this place must have been very strong," said Kiku.

" You don't really believe that nonsense? " asked Fred.

" Hush! " said Kiku sharply. " This is not the place for such talk."

They were getting close to the rocks now, and suddenly a chill, damp wind struck them. It was so cold and so unexpected that they drew back in alarm.

" The *tengu*'s breath," whispered Kiku.

" But there isn't any — " began Fred, and then he stopped, for out of the underbrush beside the path slithered an enormous snake, which passed quite close to them and disappeared on the other side of the road.

" It is the messenger of the god of the mountain," said Kiku.

After that no one said anything for a moment. " Let's get out of here," said Ernest. " I don't like this place."

Without a word they started down the path in such a hurry that Fred forgot to get out his compass and take his bearings. They kept close together, going fast. When they came to the landslide, Fred peered over the edge. " I think you made a new whirlpool," he said. " Come and see, Ernest."

But Ernest backed away, looking rather white. " I don't want to look," he said.

After that they went more slowly. But they didn't stop until they saw the thatched roof of the inn among the trees.

Fred looked back the way they had come. " All the same," he said, " I'm sure there's a good scientific reason for the wind hole. Of course," he added, " there isn't any *tengu*."

# 14..

## The Rescue

Father was feeling quite all right again. He sat at the open doorway watching a little anxiously for the boys' return. When they came into sight at last, he hurried to meet them.

"Sorry we're late," said Fred, suddenly wondering if they had done right to go off without permission. "We didn't want to disturb you when you were sick, so we went to the *Tengu's* Wind Hole. And Ernest started an avalanche —"

"I did not," Ernest interrupted indignantly. "It just happened."

Father took one look at Ernest, whose face was pale and streaked with dirt and sweat. "We'll talk about it later," he said. "Right now we'll get this boy to bed." He put an arm around Ernest and helped him into the inn.

A maid spread down a mattress and made Ernest comfortable. Only then did the boys have a chance to tell their adventures.

Father listened until he heard about the landslide. "Ernest might have been killed!" he interrupted them anxiously. " What will Mother say to this? "

" It's all right," said Ernest. " You see, I had hold of the tree."

" Then we got to the teahouse," Fred went on with the story. " It was very nice, and Kiku knew how to order the food. The old man is a carver and Kiku bought something from him."

" It is a *tengu*," said Kiku, and showed it to Father.

" It's well done," said Father. " See how the carving follows the lines of the root. The beaked nose was there already. The old man added eyes and mouth. He is a good artist."

" While the boys were in the workshop," Ernest took up the tale, " the old lady offered me medicine. It was a snake pickled in rice wine. She gave the bottle a shake, and the snake wriggled up and down. Ugh! " he finished.

" A snake! " cried Fred.

" Country people think a snake pickled in sake wine is very good medicine," said Kiku, " especially for the very old."

" I've heard of it," said Father, " but I have never come across it. What did you do, Ernest? "

" I said I wasn't worthy of such honorable medicine, and that she must keep it for herself and her husband. She was awfully kind. I didn't want to hurt her feelings."

" Certainly not," said Father. " You did quite right."

" Then," said Fred, " we went to the *Tengu*'s Wind Hole. There was a cold wind that came out of somewhere. The old man said it was the breath of the *tengu*. And the old woman said there was a snake that was the messenger of the god of the mountain. We saw the snake too. It came out while we were there. They really believe all that," he added. And remembering the cold draft of air, and the black rocks, and the big snake, he felt a little uneasy in spite of himself.

Father sighed a little. "It is sad," he said. "You see, there are so many disasters in Japan — earthquakes and tidal waves and volcanic eruptions — that poor, ignorant people think evil spirits must bring them. So they believe in ogres, and *tengus,* and fox gods, because they have never been taught any better."

By the time they had finished their story, supper was ready, and after they had eaten, Father said they must all settle down.

"We missed out on a whole day," he said. "We must get an early start tomorrow. It was my fault, because I didn't listen to Kiku-san about the shellfish. I can't blame you for going off on your own today, but after this we must keep together. Will you remember that?"

"Yes, we will," they promised.

Fred and Ernest were already asleep when Kiku spoke softly. "Poate-san," he said, "I would like to ask a little question."

"Yes, Kiku-san?" said Father.

"Perhaps there is no *tengu,*" said Kiku, "but we saw the big snake with our own eyes. Was the old woman mistaken when she said it was the messenger of the god of the mountain?"

"Yes," said Father. "The snake is just a creature who lives there. It crossed the road because that is its habit, and you happened along at the right time to see it. Do you understand?"

Kiku nodded. " Yes, Poate-san," he said, " I think I understand."

~~

They had an early breakfast and were off almost before it was light. Even so, the landlord and all the servants were on hand to say good-by and wish them good fortune on their journey.

It was not far to the mountain, and soon they were walking on a lava road that climbed up and up, winding between rocks or running beside deep ravines.

" The good mountain climber," said Father, " takes the climb slowly and steadily. He doesn't hurry and he doesn't slow down, and he straightens his knee with every step, because that rests his leg muscles." He led the way and the boys fell into step behind him, like good mountaineers.

Father was in fine spirits, flourishing his alpenstock. " U-pi-dee, u-pi-da," he sang. " U-pi-dee i-da," the boys joined in. It was great fun.

After a while they came upon the members of the pilgrim society, listening respectfully to their guide. " The snow-capped peak to your right — " he was saying in a loud voice, and all the pilgrims turned and bowed in the direction of the mountain he was talking about.

When they saw Father and the boys, they greeted them like old friends, and moved to one side to let them pass.

" We'll see you later," said the boys, and waved at them gaily.

" U-pi-dee," sang Father. But now they were interrupted by shouts and laughter as two Japanese schoolboys came racing up the trail.

Fred started to hurry. " I can go as fast as they can," he said.

" Of course," said Father. " But they're no mountain climbers. Pretty soon they'll be tired out, and we will overtake them. You'll see. Look out! " he broke off to shout a warning. The trail turned at a sharp angle, and one of the racing boys, not looking where he was going, almost fell over the cliff. Sobered a little, they turned to make a polite bow to Father before they went on more slowly.

" They ought to look where they're going," said Father.

They started on again, but everyone was getting tired. Father called a halt so that they could look around. Below them, the inn looked small and far away, and above them, snow-capped peaks rose high into the air. But here on the trail it was warm and mild, and everywhere flowers were blooming, larger and brighter-colored than they had ever seen before. Suddenly Father raised his head to listen.

" What's that? " he asked.

" Help! Help! " a faint cry came to their ears. Father rushed up the path, the boys close at his heels. " Help! " The cry was nearer now, and then around an angle in the road they came upon one of the Japanese boys who had passed them. " Help! " he cried. Then seeing Father, he bowed. " Honorable sir," he babbled, " I am Katsutoji. Shusai," he began to sob, " Shusai has fallen over the cliff." And he pointed a trembling finger.

In a moment Father had reached the edge and was

leaning over. There, only a little way down, the boy was crouching on a narrow ledge of rock, clinging desperately to the root of a pine tree. For the moment he was safe, but below him the rock fell away in a drop of many feet. There was no time to lose.

" Hold on, Shusai-san," said Father. " We'll get you."

He lay down and reached over as far as he could, but the boy was just beyond his grasp. " Hold my legs, boys," said Father, " and I'll lower the alpenstock for him to take hold of." The boys threw themselves on him: Fred and Ernest on one leg and Kiku and Katsu on the other. Then Father, holding the sharp end of the alpenstock in his hand, lowered the curved handle until it touched Shusai. But Shusai's eyes were tight shut. He gave a little yelp of fright when he felt the touch of the stick, but he didn't stir to help himself.

" Shusai-san," Father encouraged, " open your eyes. Take hold of the stick and I can pull you up."

" I can't," came a wail. " My fingers won't open. They are fastened to the tree."

Father could see that the boy's knuckles were white where he was holding on in panic. " I'll have to go down after him," he said, getting up. " If only we had a rope."

" Our sashes," cried Kiku. In a flash he had taken off his sash and handed it to Father. Katsu did the same.

" Splendid! " said Father. He knotted the sashes end to end, and looked around for something to tie the sash rope to. But there was nothing, not a tree, nor even a point of rock. " The alpenstock will have to do," he muttered, and drove the iron spike hard into a crack between the rocks. He tested it. It seemed firm. Then he tied one end of the sash rope to the alpenstock and made a loop

in the other before he lowered it over the cliff edge.

" It's long enough." He drew a breath of relief. " Now, boys, sit down and hold on to the alpenstock to ease the strain. When I get Shusai-san and give the word, pull on the rope with all your might to help us. Do you understand? Fred " — he turned to Fred as the oldest — " if anything goes wrong, you are not to try to go after me. Call for help. Will you promise me? "

" Yes, Father," said Fred soberly.

The boys got down and held on as they were told, and Father, looping the rope over his arm, lowered himself carefully over the edge. His foot, searching for a hold, let loose a shower of stones, and then found a small outcropping of rock that held his weight. Carefully he searched for another and lowered himself again, the rope growing taut with his weight. He had gained the ledge beside Shusai.

" I have you, Shusai-san," he said. " Let go of the tree."

But poor Shusai's hands were paralyzed. He could not move them. There on the narrow ledge of rock with only the loop of sash over his arm, and the drop below, Father pried each of Shusai's fingers loose and slipped the rope loop over his head and under his arms.

" Up we go. Pull, boys! " he shouted.

The boys pulled, and Father and Shusai, helped by the rope, scrambling somehow, clinging to every projection on the face of the cliff, reached a place where the boys could catch hold of them by the arms, the sleeves, the collars, and so drag them to safety.

" Well done," said Father, and sat down rather suddenly. " Thank God that's over."

# 15. .

## An Invitation

*The boys* crowded around, talking excitedly. " Are you all right? " Fred kept saying. Ernest was feeling for broken bones. Shusai had hard work to keep back the tears. He screwed his face into a dreadful frown, but his lips were trembling. There was a long scratch on his face, which Ernest examined carefully.

" We ought to have some water to wash that," he said, and dabbed it with his handkerchief.

" Don't be silly," snapped Fred, hardly knowing what he was saying. " They might have been killed and you talk about a scratch."

Father spoke calmly. " We are safe and sound, and we can be thankful for that. What we need," he went on practically, " is something to eat. It's lucky I got a half dozen rice balls at the inn this morning. There's one for each of us." He opened his bundle and took out the rice balls, each one wrapped in a blue cotton square. They were round and solidly packed, and in the center of each one was a sour red plum.

It was wonderful how much better everyone felt for eating. The boys were soon laughing together.

111

"It was like a tug of war," cried Fred with sparkling eyes. "We hauled Father and Shusai-san right over the edge. Though of course they helped us too," he added.

"You did very well," said Father.

"Are you going to the Hot Springs too?" asked Fred, turning to Shusai and Katsu.

"No," said Shusai. "We are making a pilgrimage to the shrine of Michihito farther up the mountain. We have to be home again by nightfall."

"We make the pilgrimage every year," said Katsu.

"This is the first time we have gone alone," said Shusai. "and this miserable one fell over the cliff."

"But you have learned wisdom," said Father. "The shrine of Michihito," he went on, "must be of special interest to you if you make the pilgrimage to it every year."

"Michihito was our ancestor," said Shusai. "Katsu and I are cousins. We make the pilgrimage each year as descendants of the hero."

Father stood up. "Now that we have rested," he said, "we had better start on again."

Shusai made a bow. "Honorable sir," he said, "is it permitted that we join your party? We ask it most humbly."

"We'll be glad to have you," said Father. "Isn't that right, boys?"

"Yes!" they all cried.

"It will be like the pilgrim society," Kiku added happily.

Father pulled his alpenstock out of the crack in the rocks. "No harm done to it," he said. "You boys did a good job of holding it steady."

The day was no longer pleasant. Mist covered the valley. They seemed to be above the clouds. It was cold, and the path was very steep. They went slowly, stopping often to rest. No one talked much. Katsu, who was the youngest, looked around him a little fearfully. " It is a good place for ogres to live," he whispered to Shusai.

Shusai didn't answer, for just then he saw the shrine. " There it is! " he cried. " There is the shrine of Michi-hito! "

Silhouetted against the sky were two upright wooden posts with a curved crosspiece. It was a *torii,* or gateway, to the shrine. Shusai and Katsu now went on alone, and the others waited. At the gateway they both bowed. Then they went inside the shrine, and putting down a piece of money, they rang a bell that was hanging there, bowed again, and came back to the others.

" Why did you ring the bell? " asked Fred.

" To call the spirit of the hero," said Shusai. " If we didn't ring the bell, how would he know that we had come to pay our respects? "

No one tried to answer that question.

" The landlord of the inn where we stayed last night told me there was an inn not far from the shrine," said Father. " Do you know where it is, Shusai-san? "

" Yes," said Shusai. " When we go on the pilgrimage to Michihito's shrine, we always go to the inn to eat. I will show you the way." Shusai and Katsu led the way up a fork in the road, and soon they came to an inn nestled under an overhang of rock. The landlord who welcomed them recognized Shusai and Katsu and treated them all with added respect. It was good to take off their shoes and rest, and good, too, to have a fine meal. They ate to the pleasant sound of bells, for the pilgrim society had reached the shrine of Michihito, and the bell rang again and again as they paid their respects.

" The soul of Michihito has much cheer today," said Shusai proudly.

After they had eaten, Father went out onto the veranda and the boys talked together. Shusai and Katsu and Kiku compared notes about school. When they found that Fred and Ernest studied with their mother, they were dumfounded.

" Can your mother read and write? " asked Katsu.

" Of course," said Fred. " She can even read out loud and knit at the same time. And she can sing and play the organ."

" My mother can sing and play too," said Shusai, " and

she writes poems. But these are minor accomplishments. She could not teach me. Your ways are different," he finished politely.

At last it was time for Shusai and Katsu to start for home.

" I wish you could go with us to the Hot Springs," said Ernest.

" It cannot be," said Shusai sadly. He went to where Father was sitting on the veranda and bowed so low that his head touched the floor. " To you I will always be grateful," he said. Katsu, who always followed his cousin's lead, bowed very low too.

" We'll walk back to the shrine with you," offered Fred. They all went together to the shrine, and from there they waved good-by to the boys.

The bell of the shrine had stopped ringing. The pilgrims had all done their duty by Michihito and were cooking their suppers over tiny fires of bark and twigs. They called cheerfully to each other as they worked.

" They'll soon be asleep," said Father, " so as to be up and off early in the morning. I think we are about ready to settle down too."

Back at the inn, Father took his bath — the order of bathing was well settled by now — and then it was Fred's turn. The mattresses were already spread on the floor, and Kiku lay down to wait his turn. But Ernest pulled the covers over his head and was asleep before his turn came.

" He can bathe at the Hot Springs," said Father. " While I'm waiting for you boys to settle down," he went on, " I think I'll go out and watch the moon come up. If you want me, you know where I am," he finished, and went out to the veranda.

It was quite dark. Only a faint glow showed behind the jagged mountain peaks. Then gradually a great silver disk swam into view, and the dwarf trees, the moss-covered stones, and the stone lantern in the little garden were bathed in light.

Father sat enjoying it. But it had been a long, exciting day. Perhaps he dozed. At any rate, he was startled when a sudden bustle broke out in the inn. The landlord and all his helpers were running to the gate and shouting a welcome. Then, bowing respectfully, they ushered in the guest.

The newcomer was a man of importance. His dress was sober, but it was rich, and a servant with a lantern lighted his way. A little haughtily, he inclined his head to the landlord, then looked around as though searching for someone. Catching sight of Father, he went to him quickly and bowed.

" Honorable sir," he said in the high-pitched voice of

ceremony, "permit me to make myself known to you. I am Nishima."

Father was almost too surprised to speak, but he managed to bow in return. "Nishima-san," he said, "I am honored. Permit me to introduce myself." And he murmured his name.

Nishima-san seated himself and opened his fan. "I have come," he said, gently fanning himself, "to offer my profound thanks for your honorable service."

Father was even more surprised by this speech. What could he mean? "Honorable sir," he said, "I am afraid I do not understand."

"Shusai-san is my son," said Nishima-san. He held his fan quite still.

"Oh," said Father, understanding at last. "But how did you know? The boys left here only a few hours ago."

"They told me of the rescue as soon as they reached home. I came at once to find you."

"It is a long climb up the mountain," said Father. "And it is night."

"If I had waited until morning, you might have gone on your way," said Nishima-san. "I could not rest until I had seen you. Shusai-san," he added simply, "is my first-born."

"He is a fine boy," said Father.

Nishima-san bowed his thanks. A maid knelt beside him offering tea, which he took absent-mindedly. She went away. The manservant knelt by the door, his lantern on the floor beside him. The two men were alone. The light of the moon was so bright that they could see each other clearly.

Nishima-san closed his fan and leaned forward, his eyes on Father's face. " I would count it an honor," he said, " if you would condescend to stay under my unworthy roof, so that I could show my gratitude to the rescuer of my son."

" Why, thank you," said Father. " There are four of us together: my two sons, their friend, and I. We are on a walking trip to the Hot Springs and we are staying only one night here. After the Hot Springs, we plan to go down the mountain by the other road and so home to Morioka."

" Go to the Hot Springs by all means," said Nishima-san. " When you descend the mountain by the other road, I will have jinrikishas to meet you and bring you to my unworthy home."

Father thought quickly. An invitation like this could come only once in a lifetime. He couldn't afford to miss it. The boys would be happy to see Shusai and Katsu again, and if they had a ride to Nishima-san's house it would not be too far out of their way.

" You are very kind," said Father. " We are greatly honored."

Nishima-san closed his fan and stood up. " At midday on the third day," he said, " my men will meet you at the foot of the mountain."

" But surely you will stay at the inn tonight? " said Father.

" The moon is full," said Nishima-san. " The walk is nothing. I look forward then to your coming."

He bowed and went away, his servant following him and the people of the inn running from all directions to bow in farewell to this distinguished guest.

Father sat on in silent astonishment. It was hard to believe that this aristocrat had actually invited them to stay at his house. Such things did not happen often. Of course, thought Father, a Japanese feels he must always repay a favor. But, no, Nishima-san seemed really anxious to have them come. He was a man of intelligence and refinement. We will have much to say to each other, thought Father, with a stir of pleasure.

They were up early the next morning, but not so early as the pilgrim society. Even before it was light, the pilgrims had eaten their cold rice and started on their way.

"How would you like to pay a visit to Shusai-san's house?" asked Father at breakfast.

The boys stopped eating in surprise. "When? Where does he live?" they asked.

"Shusai-san's father came last night to invite us," Father told them. "He walked all the way up here after the boys got home and told him about Shusai-san's adventure. I thought you'd like to go, so I accepted for us all. Was that all right?"

"All right!" cried Fred. "It's great. But can't we go to the Hot Springs after all?" he asked a little doubtfully.

"Oh, yes," said Father and explained the plan. "I have an idea that Shusai-san's father is a very important man. You'll have to mind your manners, boys, when we visit him."

"Don't worry about that," said Fred. "We know how to be polite."

Even while they were eating breakfast, Fred was thinking about another meal. " Be sure to bring along rice balls, Father," he said.

" How many? " asked Father.

" Two apiece," they decided.

" Then you must each carry your own," said Father. So when they started off, each bundle contained two neatly wrapped rice balls to eat on the way.

It was a pleasant day, but chilly. They started off briskly to keep up the circulation, but they soon had to slow down, because the road was so steep. They could see the snow glistening on the high peaks, which seemed to float in the clouds without any foundation. As they climbed, mist settled about them. Father went first, and the boys kept close behind him. At the very summit they came on a tiny teahouse where they stopped to rest and drink tea. A little pool of water in a basin of rock steamed and bubbled from a hidden spring, and the landlord invited them to bathe.

" It's too cold," shivered Ernest.

But the man laughed. " The sand at the bottom of the pool is hot," he told them. " Dig your fingers in too deep and you will burn them."

" We thank you for your hospitality," said Father, and put a coin on the tea tray, " but I think we must push on."

" We have been honored," said the man. He and his wife walked a little way along the road with them. After a little while they stopped and said good-by, but when the boys looked back at the turn in the road, they were still there, smiling and bowing.

Now the road dipped downward almost as steeply as it

had climbed before. The boys pushed ahead.

" Maybe it would be easier to run than to hold back,"
suggested Fred.

But Father said no. The mist had lifted, but there were
still pockets where they could scarcely see their way. It
wasn't a road to follow carelessly. At last they saw below
them what looked like a toy village.

" The Hot Springs! " shouted the boys.

" It's a long way off still," said Fred. " Let's eat."

They sat down and ate the rice balls. Rested and re-
freshed, they started on again. Sometimes the little village seemed to disappear as the road wound round the
mountains. Then it would come into sight, and each time
it looked larger. A swift stream tumbled almost straight
down the mountain and ended in a cloud of spray. The
little houses, clinging close together, climbed to meet it,
and the front door of each house seemed planted in the
back yard of the one below.

" See the bamboo pipes," said Father, as they came
into the village. " They carry the water from the hot
springs to the public bath! " The bath was right in the
middle of the main street, and there soaking up to their
necks in the steaming water sat the members of the pilgrim society.

" Do we have to take a bath out here? " asked Ernest.

" No," said Father. " We'll go to the inn and have a
bath of our own."

So they walked past the pilgrim society, whose members called out cheerful greetings as they passed. When
they came to the gate of an inn, they were received with
shouts of welcome.

# 16..

## The Archers' Tower

Servants brought them water to bathe their feet and hot tea to drink. When they were rested, they put on kimonos and a maid led them to the bathhouse. It looked almost as though the place were on fire, for billows of steam rose to the wooden roof and eddied from the open sides.

Ernest stopped short. " What's that smell? " he asked, sniffing suspiciously.

" It's sulphur in the water," Father told him.

" I don't like it," said Ernest. " It smells like rotten eggs."

" Don't be silly," said Fred. " Come on." And he led the way into the bathhouse.

Inside the building, Ernest dipped a toe in the water and hastily drew it back again. " It's too hot," he said.

Kiku slid into the water. " Go in slowly," he counseled. " You won't mind it after a minute."

" That's all right for you," said Ernest. " You like it hot. I don't really like to bathe much anyway." Again he put out a cautious toe, and Fred, who was already in the water, caught him off balance and pulled him in.

"That's enough," said Father, who was taking his time. "A-a-ah," he said, and slid into the steaming bath.

For a minute Ernest felt angry at being pulled into the water, but to his surprise the water felt wonderful. It seemed to soak out all the soreness of the long day's tramp. At first, everyone was contented to sit and soak, but pretty soon Fred stood up and began to prance about. Then Kiku and Ernest followed, and soon they were chasing and splashing each other all over the bathhouse. Father let them play, but at last he called, "Time to eat," and the boys scrambled out, put on the hotel kimonos, and headed for the hotel proper.

"I'm starving," they shouted to each other as they ran.

They ate to the cheerful clop-clop of wooden clogs, as people passed to and fro on the village street.

"May we go out and walk around too?" asked Fred.

"Of course," said Father, and stood up ready to go.

"You're not going like that?" asked Ernest.

"Why not?" asked Father, looking down at himself, "Everyone else is wearing a kimono."

"But yours is awfully short," said Ernest. And indeed it was, for Father was very tall, and the kimono had been made for a short Japanese.

Father laughed. "Come on," he said. "I don't care."

The street was gay with strings of paper lanterns, and little booths had been set up where vendors sold their wares. The members of the pilgrim society were everywhere, mingling with the crowds and joyfully spending their few coppers on souvenirs. Suddenly Ernest gave a great yawn.

"Tired?" asked Father. He had to admit it. "Tomorrow, we go to Shusai-san's house," said Father. "You'd better get a good sleep tonight."

Back at the inn, they found their beds were already spread on the floor, and soon everyone was settled for the night.

"May we have another bath before we go?" asked Ernest sleepily.

"Ho," said Fred, "so you like baths now!"

"There are baths and baths," said Ernest. But Fred didn't answer. He was already asleep.

"I can see the crossroad at the foot of the mountain," said Fred. "That's where Shusai-san's father's rickshas are going to meet us."

"I don't see any rickshas," said Ernest.

They had been on the road since breakfast, going downhill all the way. The trail was not as well traveled as the one they had taken up the mountain. It was rough and stony, and sometimes there were sheer drops of several feet. More than once at these places Father had driven his alpenstock into the ground, and they had come down one by one, holding to it for support. Once it gave way as Ernest, last in line, leaned on it. He slid the rest of the way, tearing his sleeve and skinning an elbow. They dusted him off, and Father produced a safety pin from his bundle.

"It's good Mother put in these safety pins," he said, as he pinned up Ernest's sleeve. "We don't want to turn up at Nishima-san's house looking like tramps. There now, no one would guess that there was anything wrong."

"Are you sure that Nishima-san expects us?" Ernest

asked now, as he looked at the empty crossroad below
them.

Father smiled. " He invited us," he said.

" But he didn't see us boys," Ernest pointed out.
" Maybe he changed his mind about wanting us."

At this, Kiku grew quite red in the face. " A Japanese
gentleman doesn't change his mind," he said.

" Kiku-san is right," said Father. " The word of a
Japanese gentleman can always be trusted. We were to
be met at noon and it isn't noon yet. There's plenty of
time for the rickshas to get here."

They started on again, but when they reached the foot
of the mountain and the crossroad, there was no one
there to meet them. " We're early," said Father. " We

can sit down and rest." He settled himself in the shade of a pine tree, and Fred and Ernest sat down too. But Kiku was on the alert. When a little cloud of dust appeared down the road, he jumped up. " Here they come," he cried.

But it was only a woodcutter bent almost double under a load of firewood.

" You have a good load there," said Father in answer to the man's greeting.

" I am taking it into the town to sell," said the man, and stopped to lean his load against the bank to rest.

" Do you know the house of Nishima-san? " asked Father.

" The honorable house of Nishima-san lies beyond the village," said the man, and pointed to a distant rise of ground where a castle tower stood out against the sky. " His ancestors were the lords of this district and lived in the castle. It is in ruins now, but the house of Nishima-san is not far from it."

He straightened, shifting his load to a better position. " This humble one must go if he would sell his firewood," he said, and started on his way.

" What time is it? " asked Kiku.

" Don't worry so," said Father. " It isn't noon yet."

Kiku was worried. He shaded his eyes and stared anxiously down the road. And then they heard the sound of steady foot beats as a string of rickshas came into sight, exactly on time. " They're here! " cried Kiku.

The ricksha man who was in the lead pulled up in front of Father and bowed. " We have come," he said, " to convey the honorable foreigner and his honorable sons

to the house of Nishima-san. Be pleased to enter the
humble rickshas."

Father bowed and so did the boys. They knew this was
one time to remember their Japanese manners, for these
were no ordinary ricksha men, but private servants, each
wearing on his coat the crest of his master.

Father and the boys climbed into the rickshas and were
soon bowling along at a great rate. They passed through
the town without stopping, crossed some bridges, and
turned at last down a quiet, green lane until they came
to a gate and a gatehouse. There was a little door in the
wall for everyday use, but today the great gates were open
in honor of the visitors. Servants were out to meet them,
and after they had taken off their shoes and washed they
went inside to find Shusai and his father waiting.

The house was large and seemed even larger, for all
the paper partitions had been pushed back to let in the
air. There was no furniture at all, not a chair nor a table,
only walls and floor, and in an alcove a bronze vase beneath a painted scroll.

The boys bowed as politely as they knew how, but their
eyes took in everything, even to the moon-shaped window
through which they could see the castle tower like a picture in a frame.

They all sat down on cushions on the floor and servants
brought tea. Then Shusai's mother came in, followed by
serving maids who carried in the meal on low tables
which they set before the guests. Shusai's mother bowed
and smiled, but she didn't talk, nor did she eat with them.
But she watched to be sure everybody was well taken
care of, while Father and Nishima-san talked and talked

and the boys were respectfully silent. It was over at last, and they were free to leave the house. What a relief! They found Katsu waiting outside, and now they could laugh and shout as much as they pleased.

" Shall we go to the castle? " asked Shusai.

" Yes, yes! " they cried.

" Can we go inside? " asked Fred. " The castle in Morioka isn't safe. We've never been in it."

" We can climb the archers' tower," said Shusai. " You can see all over from there. The archers' tower," he explained, " was where the defenders made their last stand. They died fighting there."

The boys climbed the narrow stairs inside the tower and came out on a sort of platform with a low wooden parapet. Below them lay the town with its thatched roofs, and beyond were the mountains rising peak on peak.

" There is the shrine of Michihito," said Shusai, pointing.

" Did he really live in the castle? " asked Kiku.

" Yes," said Shusai. " Once all this land belonged to him. Now most of it is a public park for the town."

Fred took out his compass, and the boys crowded around to look at it. " See, the needle always points north," he explained. " That is the direction of Morioka where we live. The shrine of Michihito seems to be a little west of south." He put the compass back in his pocket and went to lean over the parapet. " I wish I had a plumb line," he said. " I'd like to measure the height of this tower."

" Be careful," warned Shusai. " The parapet is old and rotten."

But he spoke too late. There was a rending sound as the ancient wood broke under Fred's weight. For a moment Fred teetered on the very edge, and then Shusai caught his arm and dragged him back.

Everyone was too frightened to say a word. Fred found his voice first. " Shusai-san," he cried, " you saved my life! "

" Your father saved mine," said Shusai.

" Then we're even," said Fred. " Shake! " and he thrust out his hand.

Awkwardly and giggling a little, Shusai put his hand in Fred's in the unfamiliar gesture, and Fred pumped it up and down. They laughed together.

" Let's all shake hands," said Ernest. " Kiku-san, Katsu-san, put your right hands on Fred's and Shusai-san's. I will too. We will swear a pact of friendship."

So they crowded together, hands clasped. " Friends! " shouted Fred. " Hurray! "

" Friends! " they repeated. " Hurray! "

Father and Nishima-san heard the boys. " That's Fred's voice," said Father, smiling. " The boys are having a good time."

The fathers were having a good time too. They had much in common. Nishima-san was a man of intelligence, eager to know about the outside world. He listened carefully to all that Father had to say, and in turn, he told many things about his own country that no foreigner could find out for himself.

# 17..

## Home-coming

The next morning Father got up early to visit the castle, but the boys were still asleep when the maid came in with their tea.

"Oh," groaned Fred, "I could sleep for another hour."

But there was no more sleep for them that morning. Soon the sliding door was pushed back again, and this time Shusai and Katsu stood there, bowing and smiling. "We have brought you an insignificant present," said Shusai. They came in then and put on the floor, one by one, three little monkeys carved out of soapstone. The first one had its paws over its eyes. "See no evil," said Shusai. The second covered his ears. "Hear no evil,"

said Katsu. The third covered his mouth. " Speak no evil," finished Shusai.

The boys examined the monkeys. Each wrinkle in the tiny paws was traced with care. They were quite perfect.

" May I have the blind one? " asked Fred, holding it lovingly in his hand.

" I would like the deaf one," said Kiku.

" That leaves the dumb one for me," said Ernest. " It's the best of all. I would rather see and hear any day."

Fred was thinking hard. He had only one treasure and it was very dear to him. But now he took the compass out of his pocket. " For you," he said, and gave it to Shusai.

" Do you really mean it? " cried Shusai.

Fred nodded. " It points north to where we live," he said, and swallowed.

Now Ernest opened his bundle. " Here is a magnet for Katsu-san," he said. See, it can pick up a nail or any piece of metal that isn't too big."

Katsu's face shone with pleasure.

It was Kiku's turn now, and he produced the *tengu's* head carved from the gnarled root. " This is for you both," he said. " It is the *Tengu* of the Wind Hole."

The boys studied the wicked, beaked face with delight. " Who is he? " asked Shusai.

So they told of their trip to the *Tengu's* Wind Hole, and the landslide, and the snake, the messenger of the god of the mountain.

" Only of course that's all imagination," explained Fred. " There's a good scientific reason for the wind hole, only I don't know what it is."

"And the snake," said Kiku, "lives somewhere near the wind hole. It just happened to go by while we were standing there."

Shusai and Katsu thought about this. "Perhaps you are right," said Shusai after a little.

⌒

Nishima-san's men were to take them in the rickshas one day's journey.

"It is too much trouble," Father had protested. But Nishima-san insisted, so Father gave in.

They walked down the lane together, Father and Nishima-san in front, the boys following along behind. "We are very grateful for all your kindness," said Father.

"It has been an honor," said Nishima-san. "I hope you will come again."

"You must come to see us," said Father. "It isn't too far. Bring the boys too."

Nishima-san was pleased. "Perhaps we will come," he said, smiling.

The ricksha men were waiting at the end of the lane, and the travelers climbed in. "Good-by, *sayonara*," they called to each other, and then they were off. The friends stood watching until a curve in the road hid them from sight. Everyone felt a little sad at the parting.

When they stopped for something to eat at noon, Ernest was still sad. "It's too bad to make friends and then lose them," he said.

"But you haven't lost them," comforted Father. "Friends are friends even when they are a long way apart. Besides, they may come and visit us someday."

At this thought Ernest brightened a little.

Fred was looking at his monkey. " Do you think we can teach Cherry this monkey trick? " he asked. " See no evil, hear no evil, speak no evil."

" He's a smart dog," said Kiku.

" You know," said Ernest, " I'll be glad to get home. I'm sure Cherry has missed us."

They stayed one more night at an inn. Nishima-san's men had gone home, but not before Father had put a folded bit of paper with money in it in each man's hand.

" Now for the home stretch," said Father, as they started out the next morning.

It was the longest day they had ever known. The sun was almost setting when, tired and hot, they reached Morioka. First they took Kiku home. At parting he grew very polite and formal.

" To you, Poate-san, and to your honorable sons, my humble thanks for this memorable trip," he said, and bowed very low.

" We were glad to have you with us, Kiku-san," said Father. " Tell your father you were a real addition to our party." Kiku blushed with pleasure.

" Come over tomorrow," called the boys, and turned their faces toward home just as a clamor of voices broke out in Kiku's house.

" They're shouting a welcome," said Father. " Soon we'll be hearing a welcome too."

" I can hardly wait," said Ernest.

Orikasa, sitting in the doorway of the gatehouse, was the first to see them. He gave a welcoming hail and came hobbling to meet them, his face wreathed in smiles.

Bunji appeared from nowhere. Then Daisy came flying down the path with Cherry at her heels. Mother wasn't far behind, and O Yuki and O Hana, with Baby-san in her arms, knelt in the doorway. They were home again.

They took turns telling their adventures. " Father got sick on shellfish," said Fred. " So we went by ourselves to the *Tengu*'s Wind Hole, and Ernest started an avalanche."

" I did not," said Ernest. " You said that before and it isn't true. You nearly fell off the roof at the archers' tower. If it hadn't been for Shusai, I'd like to know where you'd be now."

Mother looked from one boy to the other and then she looked at Father, who smiled a little ruefully. " They're home safe anyway," he pointed out.

" Father had an adventure too," said Fred. " He climbed over a cliff to rescue Shusai, and we hauled them both up with a rope made out of Kiku's and Katsu's sashes. Of course, they helped too. It was very exciting."

" I should think so," said Mother. " I don't know that I want you to go off again without me."

" There were times when we needed you badly," said Father. " Boys, I think we'd better start off at the beginning and tell all about our trip. It wasn't so wildly exciting as it sounds, you know."

So then they followed the trip step by step, not forgetting the snake medicine and the members of the pilgrim society taking their baths in the main street of the Hot Springs village.

" I gave my compass to Shusai," said Fred.

" And I gave the magnet to Katsu," said Ernest.

"But see what we got from them," said Fred, and brought out his monkey. Ernest showed his too. " Do you suppose we can teach Cherry this trick? " asked Fred. "See no evil, hear no evil, speak no evil."

"I think you can," Mother said. "And speaking of tricks, Daisy has a surprise for you. Haven't you Daisy? "

Daisy had been listening to every word that was said. But she was burning to tell something herself. She called to Cherry. He came wagging his tail and looking expectant.

"Shake hands," said Daisy, and held out her hand. Cherry put out his paw and shook hands.

"Hurray! Good dog! " shouted Fred and Ernest, and they clapped their hands. Cherry, knowing perfectly well that he was being admired, wagged his whole body with delight. Of course, the boys had to shake hands with him too, and then he offered a paw to Father. Daisy was very proud, but when Fred said, "Good work," she felt she was walking on air.

"It's good to have you all home again," said Mother.

"I'm glad to be here," said Father.

"Me too," chimed in the boys.

"It was fun," said Ernest. "But home's best, I think."

# 18..

## The Undertow

*Father* was reading aloud from *Robinson Crusoe*. The wooden shutters were not yet closed, but the portieres on their *samurai* spear poles were drawn. The clock ticked cheerfully, the student lamp cast a friendly glow, and Cherry snoozed at Mother's feet.

Father had reached the place where Crusoe, cast upon the island, was struggling to reach shore, while the waves battered at him trying to drag him back into the sea. The children sat spellbound. " ' I resolved,' " Father read,

> " ' to hold fast by a piece of the rock and so hold my breath, if possible till the wave abated and then fetched another run, which brought me so near the shore that the next wave though it went over me, yet did not swallow me up as to carry me away; and the next run I took I got to the mainland.' "

Father closed the book. " That's all for tonight," he said.

Mother laid down her knitting. " How cozy it is," she said. " I could almost think we were back in Ashtabula."

At that everyone laughed. Ohio was a long way off.

Somehow a desert island seemed closer to the children than Ashtabula.

" I wish we lived on an island," said Daisy.

" You do," said Father.

" It doesn't feel like it," said Daisy. " I wish we could see the ocean again. You promised me I could choose where to go on our holiday. Let's go to the seashore."

Father looked at Mother. He was going the next morning on a walking trip to preach in the villages. Why couldn't Mother and the children meet him at the seashore when he had finished the trip? " We could all have a holiday," he said.

Mother was delighted. " Orikasa can get us a cart and we will ride in it to meet you," she said.

The children whooped with joy. They talked and talked until Father said they must be off to bed. " At this rate, I won't be able to get up in the morning to start on my trip," he said.

Even in bed the boys kept on talking until they fell asleep, and in the morning their first words were about the seashore. Father had gone before they were awake, and Mother had breakfast waiting for them.

" Earthquake last night," said Ernest, and pointed at the clock. Sure enough it had stopped.

" Only a little one," said Mother as she started the pendulum.

In the days that followed, the boys got out their bathing suits. They were tight, but they would have to do. Mother found some blue yarn to knit a suit for Daisy. She took Father's place reading *Robinson Crusoe*, knitting as she read, her needles flying almost as though they were doing all the work by themselves.

It was decided that O Hana should go with them to help with Baby-san. O Yuki would stay home to take care of the house and Cherry.

" But Cherry has never seen the ocean," said Daisy.

" He will be happier at home," said Mother. " Dogs don't like change."

At last the great day came, and Orikasa produced the native cart and driver. But it was a disappointment. The driver was a sullen fellow, and the horse drooped in the shafts, a poor creature with a great sore on his flank. Mother looked unhappy, but it was too late to do anything about it. The children scrambled into the cart in great excitement, and O Hana with Baby-san and Mother followed. They turned to wave good-by to O Yuki and Orikasa, and suddenly the driver, who had been looking at the ground, came to life and pushed his goad into the horse's sore. With a convulsive start, the poor creature jumped forward, and everybody landed in a heap on the floor of the cart. Baby-san began to cry, and the boys laughed excitedly. But Mother spoke to the driver in a voice no one had heard her use before.

" You are not to touch that horse again," she said.

The man did not turn his head. Without a word, he tramped along beside his horse. In subdued silence they rode through the city streets, the horse going slower and slower. Again the man raised his goad.

" If you touch that horse," said Mother, " I will scream and I will have the children scream too."

The man looked at the cartload of children, already eagerly drawing in breath for the promised scream, and he hesitated. A crowd had gathered to watch the foreign lady and her children. He dropped his goad, and the horse moved slowly on.

It was fun at first, but the road was rough, and as they jolted along the trip seemed very long.

" Did Father really walk all this way? " they wondered.

How good it was to come at last to the end of the journey and to see Father waving at them. They piled out of the cart, eager to tell of their adventures. The man with the cart was to wait for their return trip, and Ernest hung back to talk to him.

" I'll see you in the morning," said Ernest after a few words with the man.

" He doesn't know any better," Ernest explained. " I told him his horse would work better if he were cured. I'm going to help him fix a poultice tomorrow."

Father smiled his approval. " Good! " he said.

It was a wonderful holiday. The weather was fine, and the children lived in their bathing suits, digging in the sand and playing in the shallow water. Father said they could not swim because of the undertow.

" It's strong enough to carry a grown man out to sea," he said.

Fred, who was a good swimmer, felt this was a great shame, but Ernest disliked the water and was perfectly satisfied. As for Daisy, she was too proud of her new blue bathing suit to want to get it wet.

On the very last day, Father suggested that he and Mother go for a tramp together.

"O Hana is in charge of Baby-san," he said. "And Fred can be junior in command. I know we can trust you all."

It started out like all the other days. O Hana and Baby-san sat on the beach, while the children built a great sand castle with a moat around it. Slowly the water seeped into the moat until it was full. Then O Hana made a drawbridge of twigs to span the moat.

"The *samurai* crossed this," she said, "when they escorted their lord, the *daimyo,* on his trip to the capital."

"Tell us some more," said the children.

"No one was supposed to look at the *daimyo* when he passed," said O Hana. "Word was sent out beforehand to all the villages that everyone must stay indoors until he had gone by. My grandmother, when she was a little girl, hid in a shed and peeped out at the procession. The *daimyo* rode in a litter, carried on the shoulders of his retainers. There were hangings of gold, and the sun glittered on the spears of the *samurai*. She never forgot, but she dared not tell what she had seen — not for years and years."

It was time now for Baby-san's nap, and O Hana took her to the house.

" I'm tired of sand castles," said Fred, and waded out into the water. The tide was going out and the water was shallow. He kept going.

" Not too far! " called Ernest.

" Fraidy cat," said Fred, and went a little farther. He might have turned back then, if Daisy hadn't called.

" Come back! " she said. " I'll tell Father."

No little sister was going to boss him. Fred ran on with a great splashing. The water was above his knees when he turned to wave a defiant hand. Suddenly a wave, so strong and fierce that it seemed almost alive, swept him off his feet. Choking and frightened he had scarcely time to get his breath before another wave seized him.

Ernest and Daisy, alone on the beach, saw it all.

" Help! Help! " they shouted, but their voices seemed small and weak.

" O Hana-san, help! " wept Daisy.

The sun was going down, and sea and sky were a lovely pale lavender, very beautiful and very lonely. There wasn't a soul in sight. The children stood and watched Fred being carried out to sea.

A wave broke over him, and they lost sight of him. Then there he was swimming hard toward shore. Another wave broke, and they were sure he was gone, but no, he was a little nearer. Forgetting to shout, almost forgetting to breathe, they watched Fred fighting his way back, sometimes hidden by a wave, then swimming with

all his might. At last he was wading, the undertow dragging at him. But he was weak and staggering. Now he was
down. The waves had him again.

" Help! " screamed Ernest.

And miraculously help was there. O Hana was flying
down the beach. She ran into the water. It was up to her
waist, tearing at her, but she never wavered. Finally she
had Fred on her back, and inch by inch she fought her
way to shore. She laid him, cold and still, on the sand.

" He's dead," wailed Daisy.

Not for nothing had Ernest studied the doctor book. He turned Fred on his stomach, his head propped side-wise on an arm, and, astride of him, he placed his out-spread hands below the ribs and pressed. Water squelched from Fred's mouth. Swing back, swing forward. Ernest forced air in and out of Fred's lungs, steadily, rhyth-mically, just as he had read in the book.

" Rub his legs," he panted. And O Hana and Daisy fell to chafing Fred's legs while tears ran down their faces.

At last Fred gave a little whimper, and slowly color crept into his cheeks. Not until he was quite sure all was safe did Ernest stop. Then, shaken and trembling, he sank onto the sand.

O Hana was on her knees, her eyes raised to heaven. " Thank you," she said in heartfelt gratitude.

But Fred was shivering now, his teeth chattering. " We've got to get him to the house," Ernest said. " Can you get up, Fred? You must." Someway, prodding and pulling, they got Fred to his feet, and, arms around him, half dragged, half carried him to the house.

" I'll get him into the hot bath," said Ernest. " O Hana-san, please make tea. And Daisy, get Father's shawl."

They flew to obey. When Father and Mother came, Fred, warmed by the bath and wrapped in the wool shawl, was sipping tea. They listened to the story.

" Oh, Fred," said Mother on a sighing breath.

" I'm dreadfully sorry," said Fred. " I never thought it would happen so quickly."

" Thank God you are safe," said Father.

After supper, they talked some more.

" I thought of Robinson Crusoe," said Fred, " how he clung to the rocks and held his breath when the waves broke over him, then ran as far as he could before another wave came. There wasn't any rock for me to hold to, but I dug my toes into the sand and held my breath when the waves came, and then I swam as hard as I could before another wave caught me. Robinson Crusoe helped save me."

" And O Hana-san," said Daisy.

Mother's arm was around O Hana's waist. " We'll never forget it," she said.

" If Ernest hadn't known what to do, Fred would never have come to life again," said O Hana.

Mother's and Father's eyes as they looked at Ernest were full of love and pride. " Daisy helped too," he said.

" Everyone helped," said Mother.

" And God, most of all."

# 19..
## The Wedding

It *is time* to make wedding plans," said Mother. " O Yuki-san, you know all the things that are proper for a wedding. You must give us your advice. We want everything just right for O Hana-san and Bunji-san."

They were sitting together in conference — O Yuki, O Hana, Mother, and Daisy. The boys were off on their own affairs. Weddings were the business of women.

Daisy was very excited. " Will you have a white wedding dress with a veil? " she asked O Hana.

" White! " cried O Yuki, and threw up her hands.

" In Japan white is for mourning," O Hana explained.

" May I be a bridesmaid? " Daisy asked hopefully.

" I'm afraid you're too young, dear," said Mother.

" There should be a young girl to assist at the marriage," said O Yuki, who couldn't bear to have Daisy disappointed.

" Please, there is no girl I like so much as Daisy," said O Hana.

" Please! " cried Daisy.

" All right," said Mother, smiling. " If O Hana-san is willing, you may. Now, O Yuki-san," she went on, " we

146

must get things planned. What must the bride have in her dowry? I will write it all down, as you tell me. Poate-san and I want to do everything properly and in order."

"First," said O Yuki, counting importantly on her fingers, "a bureau for her clothes. Then a desk for writing."

"A desk?" asked Mother, surprised.

"Yes," said O Yuki firmly. So Mother wrote it down. "A workbox," O Yuki went on, "and two lacquer trays, or perhaps tables, with all the furnishings: cups, bowls, and chopsticks." She paused.

"Yes," said Mother, writing busily.

"Bedding," said O Yuki. "At least two sets. And clothes for all seasons of the year. Many sashes. Sometimes," she grew expansive, "a bride will have enough clothes to last her lifetime."

"Oh, no," said O Hana, shocked at such extravagance.

"Well," O Yuki admitted, "that, of course, is for the very rich."

"Is that all?" asked Mother at last, when she had written down everything.

"Yes-s." O Yuki hesitated. Mother was going to ask her again, but Daisy was talking.

"May I have a new dress for the wedding?" she asked.

"Of course," said Mother, and she wrote that down too.

"What color?" asked Daisy.

"What would you like?"

Daisy thought for a while. "Blue," she decided. Mother promised they would get material for the bridesmaid when they shopped for the bride.

That evening she showed the list to Father. " Do you think it is all right? " she asked.

" Very good as far as it goes," said Father. " But where are the gifts for the bridegroom's family? "

" O Yuki never mentioned them," said Mother.

" It would be embarrassing for her," said Father. " She is the mother of the bridegroom."

" Of course," said Mother, and remembered now O Yuki's hesitation about adding to the list.

" The bride must give a present to the bridegroom and to all members of his family. " That means Bunji and O Yuki, yes, and Orikasa."

" What kind of presents? " Mother asked.

" I think silk would be suitable for Bunji and his mother. You might consult O Hana about a gift for Orikasa."

" I will," said Mother. " But the poor girl is overwhelmed already. I doubt if she will have any suggestions."

Yet when Mother asked O Hana, she did after all have an idea. Silks for Bunji and O Yuki would be very fine, she said, and for Orikasa, she would like a charcoal heater, because his old bones minded the cold. Unless, of course, O Hana added, it was too much to ask of their kindness.

" It's a lovely idea," said Mother, and wrote down, " Charcoal burner for Orikasa."

Bunji brought his gift for O Hana, a splended sash, very long and shot with gold. " It is long," he said. " May our life together be long and happy," and he smiled at O Hana.

No one was without a needle and thread in the days that followed. All three women sewed for O Hana, and besides, Mother was making Daisy a blue dress with hem-stitched ruffles.

Daisy put on airs in front of the boys. " I'm going to be a bridesmaid," she kept saying.

They didn't want to be left out. " What can we do at the wedding? " they asked.

" You can be ushers," Mother said, " and stand at the door to welcome people and bring them in. It is very important that the guests feel at ease."

" We ought to give them a wedding present," said Fred one day. " How much money have we got? "

They counted it out. There wasn't much.

" What can we buy with it? " they asked.

Mother considered. " How about a teakettle? " she asked.

They spent a long time shopping. Even common things for everyday use were pretty. At last they found what they wanted, a squat little kettle with a raised design of radishes.

" It's lovely," said O Hana. " Every time I make tea, I will think of you."

When Kiku came for his English lesson, they showed him the teakettle.

" I would like to give a present too," he said. And the next day he brought a carved sandalwood fan, which filled the room with its fragrance. O Hana could scarcely speak her thanks. The boys were pleased.

" We're to be ushers at the wedding," they told Kiku. " Do you want to help? It's all right, isn't it, Mother? " they turned to her.

" It would give us pleasure," said Mother, and Kiku's smile told them it would give him pleasure too.

Now the bride's dowry was ready, each piece carefully done up in a wrapping cloth waiting to be carried to the gatehouse.

" Bunji can take them anytime," said Mother.

O Yuki was shocked. " The bridegroom cannot carry the dowry," she said.

" But who will, then? " asked Mother.

" Hired bearers from the city," said O Yuki. " And Orikasa-san, as the go-between who first proposed the match, will go before the bearers to lead the way."

" I am glad you told me," said Mother. " Poate-san will ask Orikasa-san to make the arrangements. All must be well done for our O Hana-san."

" How can I thank you for all this kindness! " cried O Hana.

" We do it because we love you," said Mother. " If you think we are kind, just pass the kindness on to someone else."

" All my life I will do it," promised O Hana.

That night at evening prayers, Father invited everyone to come the next day to the wedding of O Hana and Bunji. All over the room there rose a happy hiss of indrawn breaths. On the way home, little groups stopped to talk of it. Many of them were very poor. This could happen only once in a lifetime. It would be a red-letter day.

Early the next morning, a great hubbub broke out in the courtyard. The bearers had come to take the bride's possessions to the home of the bridegroom. Orikasa shouted orders and changed them, the men laughed and poked and jostled each other. All was confusion. But, at last, the bureau, the desk, the workbox, the tables, and all the other things in their wrapping cloths had been shouldered, and the bearers were ready to start. Orikasa put himself at their head.

" May we go too? " shouted the boys. Mother nodded.

And off they started, the boys walking with Orikasa, and the bearers following in a long line. It was a fine procession. O Yuki stood proudly counting the men, and O Hana peeped from the doorway.

" It's such a little way to the gatehouse," said Ernest. " No one will see us at all."

" I've decided that we will go to the rock where the little tree grows and back by way of the castle," said Fred.

" But that is out of our way and very far," protested Orikasa.

" We walk it every day," said Fred. " It's not far. Everyone knows us along the way. They ought to see O Hana-san's wedding procession."

Orikasa did not know how to say no, and before he realized it they were past the gatehouse and on the city street. People turned to look at them.

" Old man," someone called to Orikasa, " whose bridal procession is it? "

" It is O Hana-san's," beamed Orikasa, " she who lives at the house of the foreigner."

" It is a fine procession with many bearers," said another. " It must be that the foreigner holds her in high regard."

At that Orikasa held his head high and the boys felt very proud. In the crowd were many they knew.

" Good morning," the boys called to them. " A fine day for a wedding."

They had a splendid time. So did Orikasa. When they finally reached the gatehouse, he said they had done well to take the long way. It had done honor to the bride and also to the honorable master.

When it was time for the wedding, the boys stationed themselves at the door to welcome the guests. Fred and Ernest were very polite, but it was Kiku who made the lowest bows, even to those who were very poor.

O Yuki, behind the sliding paper doors, waited for the music so that she could start the bridal party on its way. Daisy looked down at her bouquet of chrysanthemums.

" I'm shaking," she whispered. " I can't stop."

O Yuki looked at the flowers too. " It is as though a little breeze played over the chrysanthemums," she said.

Then Mother began the music, and Father and Bunji took their places. O Yuki pushed back the sliding door, and Daisy led the way, her cheeks very pink and her eyes like stars.

A little behind her came the bride. Her eyes were downcast, and her steps so tiny that she seemed to float to her place beside Bunji.

" Dearly beloved," said Poate-san, " I am going to tell you the story of a wedding when Jesus was here on earth." He told them the story of the marriage in Cana of Galilee. " Though we cannot see him," he said, " Jesus is here with us too, blessing the marriage of these, his dear children."

After the service came the feast, when everyone grew relaxed and happy. But when it was time to escort the bride to her new home, a constraint fell on the company. Orikasa led the way, with O Hana and Bunji behind him, and after them the family and guests. They started in silence. Then Mother began to sing. The native music was sad, and no one could march to it. But this was different. " Jesus Loves Me! This I Know " they sang, and their wooden clogs beat out the rhythm. Happy and singing, the bride, escorted by her friends, came to the house of her husband.

# 20..

## Company

I *wish* something nice would happen," said Fred.

Now that the excitement of the wedding was over the boys didn't know what to do with themselves. O Hana came up to help with the work every morning, but in the afternoon she went home to do her own work. Daisy and Baby-san often went with her. Daisy was fascinated with the workings of the new household. But Fred and Ernest were not interested in the bride's housekeeping. Kiku was busy at school and the boys were left pretty much to themselves.

" It will be different when we get to America," said Fred. " We'll be in school every day, and there will be plenty of boys to play with."

They were sitting beside the teahouse when their attention was attracted by a commotion at the gate.

" Someone's coming! " Ernest cried. Two rickshas passed through the gate and came up the path to the house. Never before had the boys seen such a thing. People who came to see them always came on foot. They raced to meet the newcomers.

Shusai jumped from the second ricksha. " Katsu-san

couldn't come, but I'm here," he cried. " Friends! Hurray! "

" Friends! " cried Fred, and seized the hand that Shusai offered.

" Friends! " cried Ernest, and put his hand on top of theirs. " Hurray! " they shouted together.

Nishima-san was getting out of the other ricksha. Fred hurried to greet him. " Be pleased, honorable sir, to enter our unworthy home," he said. " Mother! " he lifted his voice. " Mother! Company! "

Mother came to the door, her knitting in her hand. What she saw was a richly dressed Japanese gentleman, a small Japanese boy, and in the background two rickshas with their runners. It was a scene of greater elegance than the house had known since the days of the *daimyos*.

" Mother, Nishima-san and Shusai-san have come to see us," said Fred.

Mother bowed. " Nishima-san," she said, " this is an honor. Be pleased to enter with your honorable son."

Nishima-san murmured politely and stepped into the house.

" Boys," Mother turned to them, " please take the ricksha men back to O Yuki and ask her to make tea for them and bring us some."

Fred and Ernest and Shusai beckoned to the men and led them around the house, and Mother turned to Nishima-san. There were always cushions on the floor for the Japanese guests, who preferred them to chairs. Mother pushed one forward and sat down on another.

" My husband has not come back from the university," she explained, " but I expect him soon. He will be very glad to see you. He has spoken often of you and of Shusai-san."

Nishima-san bowed. He was not used to conversation with women, least of all with foreign women. But he showed no sign of surprise when Mother sat down prepared to chat with him as an equal. The boys came back and sat down too. Here at home they were not afraid to talk, and soon everyone felt at ease.

Shusai showed the compass. " It guided us all the way here," he said.

Mother had been expecting O Yuki to bring the tea, but no tea appeared, and after a little she slipped away to see what was the matter. She found O Yuki in a state

of great excitement and muttering to herself.

" He is a very great lord," she said to Mother. " The men have told me. His ancestors — "

" I know," said Mother, " but we must give him tea. Please, O Yuki-san, calm yourself."

O Yuki picked up the teakettle and then she put it down again. " Did you see the crest embroidered on the ricksha men's coats? " she asked. " Truly, this is a great honor to our house."

" He is an important man," said Mother, " but he is also Poate-san's friend. He must be well treated. Please, O Yuki-san, make the tea."

O Yuki picked up the teakettle. " The men have gone into the city for the night," she said. Then, seeing Mother's look, she began to pour out the hot water, but not into the teapot — into the little cups instead. " Oh, now," she cried, " forgive the foolish one," and at last she made the tea.

" I'll go back now," said Mother. " Please bring in the tea as soon as I am seated."

At the very thought, O Yuki gave a loud groan. " Please, I cannot do it," she cried. " My old knees would give way before such honorableness."

" Nishima-san is so used to being waited on that he won't notice at all who serves him," said Mother.

But O Yuki still shook her head, and laughing a little, Mother took the tray and went back to the others.

They were all talking in a friendly way and sipping tea when the Swiss clock began to strike. Nishima-san and Shusai looked up in pleased surprise, and Mother, as always, felt a glow of pride in the clock.

" It's a Swiss clock," said Fred, " that strikes the hour. Switzerland has mountains too. It's where Father got his alpenstock," he said, turning to Shusai.

" Is it permitted that I look at honorable clock? " asked Nishima-san.

Mother nodded, smiling, and Nishima-san went over to examine it. " Does it tell time both day and night? " he asked.

" Yes," said the boys. " It only stops when there is an earthquake," Ernest said.

The clock was such a success that Fred decided to show the other things, just as O Yuki did to visitors.

" This is the cabinet the Emperor Meiji gave Father when he left the university. See, the little doors open and there are secret drawers inside." He pulled them out one by one.

" Allow me," said Nishima-san, " to contemplate the Mikado's cabinet for a little." He sat down before it in silence.

This was Mother's chance. She knew from experience that the Mikado's cabinet was good for a long time of contemplation. She picked up the tea things and hurried to the kitchen. How in the world, she wondered, was she going to take care of this great man in her simple household?

But she didn't need to worry. When she slid back the paper door, she saw O Yuki preparing vegetables. Daisy was feeding Baby-san, and O Hana, the cause of all this peace and quiet, was cooking dinner.

" O Hana-san! " cried Mother. " How glad I am to see you."

O Hana smiled. " When we saw the rickshas," she said,

"we came as soon as we could. There will be much to do."

"I should think so," said Mother. "Poate-san and the boys had a wonderful time at the house of Nishima-san. I do want him to be comfortable here."

"I have thought it all out," said O Hana. "We will serve him Japanese-style, just as he is used to."

"I haven't low tables, or Japanese beds," said Mother.

"I have," cried O Hana. Her eyes were shining. "You gave them to me. Now I can use them for you. We have already brought the trays and dishes. O Yuki-san and I are preparing Japanese-style dishes. Bunji will bring the mattresses after prayers tonight. All will be well done. The honorable visitors can live as they are accustomed."

"Dear O Hana-san," said Mother. "You have thought of everything. How can I thank you?"

"It is only the smallest part of what you have done for me," said O Hana.

Nishima-san was still contemplating the Mikado's cabinet when Father came pedaling up the path.

"Here's Father," said Fred, much relieved. The boys had been talking by themselves at one end of the room, but it was not much fun with Nishima-san there. With Father home, they could go off and have a carefree time.

Nishima-san turned from the cabinet. "What is the two-wheeled thing he rides?" he asked.

"It's a bicycle," said Fred. "It came from America."

Nishima-san repeated the word, only it didn't sound much like "bicycle."

"Father, we've got company!" called the boys, running to meet him.

Father got off his bicycle and leaned it against the side

of the house. The boys led the way inside.

"Nishima-san!" he cried delightedly. "This is a pleasure. And Shusai-san. How glad I am to see you!"

Nishima-san was all smiles, and Shusai bowed so low his forehead touched the floor. Father sat down on a cushion, and they fell to talking as though they would never stop.

Fred slipped out to the kitchen. "Mother," he asked, "may we go and get Kiku?"

"Yes," said Mother. "Bring him back with you for supper. Only be sure to get home in good time."

"Somebody take Baby-san," said Daisy. "I'm going too."

So O Hana took Baby-san, who went to her good-naturedly, not minding at all as long as she was fed.

Shusai and Ernest were waiting at the kitchen door. "Shusai-san," said Fred, "this is our sister, Daisy."

"Hello," said Daisy in a friendly way.

Shusai was surprised to find a girl was going with them, but the boys seemed to take it for granted, so he smiled too. "Friends! Hurray!" he said, which was all the English he knew.

—

"The two-wheeled bicycle," said Nishima-san to Father, "do you ride it every day?"

"Yes," said Father. "It takes me over level ground faster than a ricksha. Of course, on the hills it is not so good as a man. But in the city it does splendidly."

"Please," said Nishima-san, "is it permitted that I examine it?"

"Come on," said Father, happy to show off his bicycle.

" When you work the pedals, the wheels turn. It's a great invention."

" It does not stand alone," said Nishima-san. " Why does it stay upright when you ride it? "

" It's the momentum," explained Father. " Once you learn to balance the thing, it goes like the wind."

" Please — " began Nishima-san, and stopped. But he looked so eager that Father guessed what he was going to say.

" Want to try it? " he asked.

Nishima-san gave an excited little laugh and nodded.

" At first you may have a little trouble balancing," said Father. " I'll call Bunji, and we will hold you up until you get the hang of it."

" Oh, I wouldn't trouble you," said Nishima-san politely.

But Father didn't pay any attention. " Bunji-san," he called. And Bunji, who was working nearby with half an eye on what was going on, came running.

" Nishima-san," said Father, " this is Bunji-san, our right-hand man."

Bunji, blushing with pleasure, bowed very low, and Nishima-san, a little surprised at being introduced to a servant, bowed too.

Father looked at his guest's pleated divided skirt. " You'll have to pull up your skirt someway," he said, " or it will catch in the bicycle chain."

So Nishima-san tucked his divided skirt into his sash, climbed to the seat of the bicycle, and put his feet on the pedals. They started slowly, but Father and Bunji were much better at holding up the bicycle than Kobi and

Akio had been. Besides, there was no canal to worry about. Nishima-san began to pedal faster. " Ha-ha! " he laughed. " This is very good."

" I think you can go alone now," said Father after a while. He and Bunji let go, and down the path sailed Nishima-san, laughing like a schoolboy. At the gatehouse he fell off, but he was soon up and, turning around, rode back to them. " Ha-ha," he laughed. " Excellent, happy ride. Ha-ha! "

# 21..

## *"Excellent, Happy Visit"*

I*'m sure* that Kiku will be home from school by now,"
said Fred, as he and Shusai, Ernest and Daisy started off
together.

It wasn't often that they went into the city by themselves. It was fun dawdling along and looking at all the
sights, especially with Shusai, who knew only village life
and was entranced with everything he saw.

Kiku was home and delighted to see them. " Come on,"
said Fred. " Mother says for you to come home to supper
with us."

Kiku sped away to get permission, and then they started
back by way of the castle. " It isn't as good as yours,"
Fred told Shusai. " There isn't any archers' tower and it's
so tumbled down that you can't go inside."

When Shusai reached the castle, he was polite, but it
was plain he was not impressed. It was one thing for them
to speak slightingly of their castle and quite another to
find someone who didn't appreciate it.

" The water lilies in the moat are very pretty," said
Daisy loyally.

" I think we ought to cross the bridge," Fred said suddenly. " It's probably much better inside than it looks from here."

" No," said Daisy. " You know O Hana never let us."

Somehow Fred could never bear to have Daisy tell him not to do anything. Now he shot a defiant look at his sister and started across the bridge. He went carefully, testing each step before trusting his weight on it. It really looked as though he might make it, when all of a sudden the planks gave way and he sank right in above his knees. The moat might look pretty with the water lilies floating on the top, but underneath it was thick, black slime. Fred turned around and started back, but the bridge had disappeared and he had to wade to shore.

" Give me a hand," he said. " Can't you see I'm stuck? " So they reached over and pulled him out. But what a sight he was, plastered with mud which had a horrid smell.

" Phew! " said Ernest and held his nose.

" I guess we'd better go home," said Fred.

" Maybe we'd better hurry," said Daisy. " You'll have to get cleaned up before supper." But she didn't say, " I told you so."

They broke into a jog trot, not saying anything at all. But Shusai noticed that Daisy had no trouble in keeping up with the boys. When they got home, Daisy took charge.

" We'll go to the back door," she said, " and, Fred, take off your shoes and stockings before you go in."

Very meekly Fred sat down and did as he was told. But when he went into the kitchen there was still a great deal of mud on him and he didn't smell very nice.

" What in the world! " cried Mother when she saw him.

" I had a little accident," said Fred. " I'll get cleaned up right away."

" Hurry," said Mother. " Supper's almost ready." So Fred hurried, and when supper was ready he was ready too, with clean clothes and nicely slicked hair.

They all sat on cushions on the floor, and Father said grace. Then O Hana slid back the paper door and bowed very low before she came into the room. She placed the low tables in front of the company and served the food very carefully with many bows of politeness.

It was a real Japanese meal, as fine as the one at Nishima-san's house, or so the boys thought. It was more fun, too, for everyone talked, and Nishima-san, still elated over the bicycle ride, laughed a great deal as he told the others about it. O Yuki, standing in the doorway listening, laughed too.

" Is there perhaps another excellent, happy bicycle in

America? " Nishima-san asked Father.

" Yes, many of them," said Father.

" Please, would it be possible to obtain one for unworthy self? " asked Nishima-san.

" I could order one from the catalogue, if you like," offered Father.

" The catalogue? " questioned Nishima-san.

" It's a big book with pictures of all kinds of things," Fred explained. " You choose what you want and send for it, and after a while it comes. It's quite easy. We got our express wagon that way."

" After supper you shall look at it," said Father.

So when things were cleared away, Fred brought the catalogue, and Nishima-san pored over the pictures of bicycles. He could not make up his mind, so Father showed the one like his own and translated the description into Japanese, because, of course, Nishima-san could not read the English.

" Very nice," said Nishima-san. " And now what presents do we give this catalogue in order to receive the honorable bicycle? "

Father explained about the cost, and Nishima-san made the proper payment. " I will write for the bicycle," Father promised. " All you have to do is to wait. It will take some time for it to come, you know."

Nishima-san bowed his thanks, but he did not want to put down the catalogue. " What is this? " he kept asking as he turned the pages filled with pictures of tables and chairs, carriages and whatnots. The children took turns reading the descriptions, and Nishima-san, Shusai, and Kiku looked and listened.

" Taboret with onyx top," read Daisy. " That means a little table."

" Can you read? " asked Shusai in surprise.

" Of course," said Daisy. " And I know the multiplication tables too."

" She's a smart girl," said Fred. It was praise that made Daisy blush with pleasure.

They were still looking at the catalogue when Bunji's voice floated through the window, chanting the call to prayers.

" We are going to have evening prayers," said Father. " Nishima-san and Shusai-san, we ask you to join us."

Nishima-san bowed and opened his fan. Fred put away the catalogue, Father lighted the student lamp, and Mother sat down at the organ. The members of the little congregation came in quietly. Anywhere else, they might have been overawed by the presence of this noble stranger, but not here. In this place they felt at home and safe. Mother began to play a hymn. Singing was the happiest thing in the world. After a little even Shusai joined in. Father told them the parable of the sower, and Nishima-san held his fan quiet while he listened.

When the services were over, they had tea together, and then everyone went home. Now Bunji appeared with the mattress beds, and O Hana made them up for the guests. Soon everyone had settled down for the night.

" It went off very well," said Father to Mother.

" It couldn't have been better," she answered.

Shusai and his father were to leave in the morning, so the children were up early, taking turns with the express

with two bronze elephant heads for handles. Everyone exclaimed over it.

" It has been in our family for many years. May your family increase and be as lasting as the bronze of the *hibachi*," said Nishima-san.

" And may our friendship be as warm as the fire that burns within it," said Father. It was a speech that seemed to please Nishima-san, who bowed very low in answer.

Now it was Father's turn to offer a present. " I would like to give you this little book," he said. " It is the gospel, the good news, and I myself have helped to revise the translations of it. I hope you will read it and that Shusai-san will too. For in it are the words of eternal life."

" Many thanks for most honorable present," said Nishima-san. " We will read it diligently."

They all walked to the gatehouse to start the guests on their way. O Yuki and O Hana and Bunji came too, and even Orikasa hobbled out to see them off.

Nishima-san and Shusai stepped into the waiting rickshas. " Many thinks for excellent, happy visit," said Nishima-san.

" Good-by, come again," everyone called.

" Friends! Hurray! " shouted Shusai. They were gone.

" It was wonderful," said Mother. " Everyone was so good and helpful. And O Hana lent us everything she had, so that we could make them feel at home. I am so thankful."

" ' Cast thy bread upon the waters,' " quoted Father, " ' for thou shalt find it after many days.' "

# 22..

## *Sayonara*

Summer had come again, and soon they would be leaving for America. They told Kiku of their plans.

" Are you really going away? " he asked. His face was very sad. " Who will teach me English? " he asked after a minute.

" Someone else is coming to live in the *daimyo*'s house," said Fred. " He will teach in the university and you can study English with him."

" Yes," said Kiku. But for the rest of his visit he was very quiet. The boys didn't feel like talking either. It had not occurred to them before that they were leaving behind everything they really knew. They had heard of America all their lives, but it was far away. They were going to leave O Hana and Bunji and O Yuki and Orikasa and Kiku and the little teahouse and the castle —

" What is to become of Cherry? " asked Kiku.

" Cherry will go with us," said Fred quickly. But even as he said it, a dreadful doubt came into his mind. There was a long sea voyage to be taken and a trip across the continent of America. How would a dog like that? It was a question one couldn't ask — not just yet anyway.

Cherry, as though he knew something was wrong, came and pushed his wet nose into Fred's hand, and then he lay down, looking at them mournfully.

"What about Cherry?" Fred put the question that night. The children looked at Mother and Father, but they knew the answer.

"I'm afraid Cherry will have to stay behind," said Mother gently. "He would be miserable on the long trip. He'll miss you, but O Hana and Bunji are his friends, and the new people who are coming will be good to him."

"But the new people haven't any children, and he's used to children," said Ernest.

"He's a trick dog," said Daisy. "They won't appreciate him."

"I know how you feel," said Mother.

The only thing to do was to be especially kind to Cherry. They petted and praised him from morning until night.

"Why don't you go to the shops?" said Mother one day. "Look for something to remember Morioka by. Each of you may choose something for a keepsake." It was the best idea anyone had thought of in a long time.

On the way, they stopped at the gatehouse as they always did. Fred was in charge of the daily walks now, for O Hana had other things to do these days. There was a new baby at the gatehouse. His name was Thomas after Poate-san, which had pleased Father very much. He was a good baby. Tied, snug and warm, on his mother's back, he slept most of the time, his little black head bobbing as she walked. When he was awake he stared at the world through black eyes as bright as shoe buttons.

" How is Thomas-san? " asked Daisy, but Thomas-san, as usual, was fast asleep.

" Come with us, O Hana-san," they begged. " Help us pick out souvenirs to take to America."

They hardly expected her to come, but she looked at them and then called to Orikasa to tell him she was going out. It was like old times, only better. Baby-san was big enough to ride in the express wagon. She was very happy to go, and laughed and chattered, pointing a fat finger at all the sights along the way. Daisy, leading Cherry, walked on one side of the wagon and O Hana on the other, while little Thomas-san slept peacefully on his mother's back.

They spent a long time at the shop, and Thomas-san obligingly slept through it all.

" Look at this old man of the sea," said Fred, holding up the model of an old man riding on the back of a fish. " It makes me think of the Festival of Sons. I'm going to take him."

Ernest was looking at a pouch made of little lacquer boxes strung on cords, each box fitting neatly into the one next to it. " It's a medicine kit," he said. " Each one of the boxes will hold a different kind of pill. This is what I want. What are you going to take, Daisy? "

" I want something pretty," said Daisy. At last she chose a little red vase sitting on its own teakwood stand. " But what about Baby-san? " she asked. " She's too little to choose a souvenir for herself. Won't you please help us, O Hana-san? "

So O Hana chose an inlaid plaque of blue with a pattern of birds and flowers. " It's blue like Baby-san's eyes," she said.

They were happier than they had been for a long time. " I will remember this day always," said O Hana.

Later that day, Fred saw Kiku coming up the path. " It's Kiku," he called to Ernest and Daisy. " Let's ask him now."

They nodded soberly. Fred took a deep breath. " Kiku-san," he said, " how would you like to have Cherry for your dog? "

It wasn't a spur-of-the-moment idea. They had talked it all over, and it seemed the best plan for Cherry.

Kiku's face lighted up. " Do you mean it? " he cried eagerly.

Daisy had a lump in her throat. "He'll be happier with you than with anyone else," she said.

~~

There was no need to find rickshas to make the trip to the port city. The railroad had come to Morioka. A crowd had gathered at the station to see them off — Bunji and O Hana, with Thomas-san on O Hana's back, O Yuki and Orikasa, and all the other friends. Kiku was there too, and his father.

They said good-by to everyone, and then Fred put Cherry's leash into Kiku's hand. "Shake hands, Cherry," he said, and Cherry put up his eager paw. "Take care of him," said Fred, and his voice trembled a little.

Daisy and Ernest each gave Cherry a hug and then clambered aboard the train. After them came Mother and Father with Baby-san. They leaned from the window to get a last glimpse. Kiku was hugging Cherry and waving. Everyone was waving. Many were in tears, but they smiled because they did not want the travelers to be sad. Mother was crying and Father blew his nose hard. The train gave a jerk and started to move. Above the noise of the engine the voices of their friends floated through the window.

"*Sayonara*," they called. "Good-by — God bless you."

# Biography of Elizabeth P. Fleming

ELIZABETH P. FLEMING was born in Morioka, Japan, of missionary parents, the first foreign baby in that region. She came to this country while still young and received her education in the United States. But the land of her birth has always held a peculiar charm for her, so that she has kept up her contacts and has done extensive research on the subject.

All the incidents in the book are true and have been told and retold in the family before they were written down. The " gift from the Mikado," a beautiful lacquer cabinet, is in the home of a doctor brother in North Carolina. A bronze *hebachi*, or charcoal burner, also mentioned in the story, was taken by another brother into a Japanese internment camp where he spent the years of the war. It is now with him in England.

Mrs. Fleming was graduated from Teachers College, Fredonia, New York, and taught school until her marriage, when she moved to Chicago. She now lives in Oak Park, Illinois. She is a ceramic artist with a kiln in which she fires her own pieces. She likes to garden, to play the piano, and to sew. Her favorite hobby is designing and embroidering gay animals on squares, which she pieces together into picture-book quilts for children in the hospital.

A widow, Mrs. Fleming has a son and daughter who grew up on these stories of Japan.